THE PATIENT'S LIST

*A gripping psychological thriller
with a killer twist*

James Caine

ISBN-13: 9798355219109
ISBN-10: 1477123456

Cover design by: Juan Padron
Library of Congress Control Number: 2018675309
Printed in the United States of America

Prologue

Amy, always know that your mother loves you. I will do anything to make sure you have a better life than I had. I will do anything to protect you.

No matter what happens, always know that everything I do, I do for you.

No matter what happens, never say a word.

CHAPTER 1

Rina Kent smiled as her handsome husband walked down the stairs to greet her in the kitchen. They were already running late for their shift at the hospital, but Rina made him a grand breakfast. Being newly married, she knew the giddy feelings for Jonas would lessen over time, at least that's what she heard from her married friends. She would try not to worry about the eventual lows they would have and focus on how happy she was in the moment.

"Good morning, Dr. Kent," Jonas said playfully, coming up behind her, firmly squeezing her rear, and kissing her neck. Rina sighed. If they weren't running late, she would try and get more of what she had this morning.

She turned and kissed her husband. "Good morning, *Dr. Kent.*" Her smile grew and they kissed again.

"Whatever you're whipping up smells amazing," Jonas said. "We need to scarf it down though. We're—"

"Going to be late, I know. I couldn't help myself."

Rina took off a few pieces of sizzling bacon and added it to the container. Denzel, their brown miniature poodle puppy, rubbed up against Rina's ankle, barking. Denzel, whose last name would be Washington if he required one, was the first gift Jonas surprised Rina with after they moved in together. For their wedding they trained him to walk down the aisle with the wedding bands. Thankfully they trained him well.

Jonas grabbed a piece of bacon from the covered bowl and ripped off half, giving it to him. "We should take separate cars today. I think I'll be done at the ER a little later than you. Try not to stay too late on the ward. The flight is in ten hours. We need to be at the airport at least three hours before."

Rina laughed. "Three hours! That's way too long to be at the airport. Don't worry," she said, palming her husband's face, "we won't miss the flight to our honeymoon."

"Two weeks in Aruba," he said with a devilish smile. "The first twenty-four hours, I want you to wear nothing. Promise?"

Rina kissed him again, taking her time to feel his soft lips. "An easy one to keep."

Jonas bent down and patted Denzel. "Sorry, boy, you're not coming." Denzel didn't appear to care, nearly smiling while being pet.

They ate their breakfast quickly. Rina brought some of it to her car and ate on the road. Luckily, they only lived ten minutes away from the hospital. Still, somehow, she found herself nearly late for her shift often.

She parked her car in the Holy Saints staff lot. She rolled her eyes when she noticed that Jonas was already parked in his designated spot for ER doctors neat the entrance. Even though he left after she did, he always seemed to find a way to get where they were going before her.

A nurse walked towards her vehicle and waved. Rina smiled and waved back to her. She felt terrible, forgetting her name. Vanessa, she thought. Or was it Valorie? Whatever her name was, she had seen her in the halls at the hospital, turning a few of her male colleagues' heads as she walked by. A blond bombshell, Rina believed was the term.

Rina was pretty, she knew, but sometimes when she observed the beauty of those a little younger, a little fitter than her, it somehow made her feel insecure. It could be that she turned thirty last month, and she knew her body would continue to change, be less... beautiful.

Rina looked at her watch and started to quicken her pace. She entered the four-storey hospital and made her way quickly past the greeting staff to the elevators.

She grimaced when she saw that they were out of order, again. How many times had Rina needed to take the stairs in this old building? She looked back towards the visitor's information desk. Displayed proudly was a sign showing that the construction of the new hospital had started, and someday in the near future, Holy Saints would be demolished. Rina might clap when that day came. She had only been working as a psychiatrist for a few years, and only one of those at Holy Saints. The building was past its prime decades ago.

Once she'd made her way up the stairs to the fourth floor, she inhaled deeply, trying to catch her breath before opening the door.

When Rina entered her floor, she waved at the new security guard, Ryan. Ryan was a tall young man, with a stubble beard. The truth was that she didn't much like him. She had caught him more than once sleeping in his office when she popped in to ask a security question regarding a patient. Night shifts were brutal, Rina knew, but sleeping on the job when he was sometimes the only person that could catch a patient sneaking off the psych ward made her pissed beyond belief. What would happen if someone got away? Patients' safety on her ward was extremely important for Rina.

Most of the time Rina would only greet him good morning or good night but today he smiled at her.

"Congratulations!" he said.

"Thanks, Ryan," Rina said. He waved his security pass at the door system, and the red light above the psych ward door turned green, then back to red instantly. "Door's having problems again?"

"Nothing works at this hospital," Ryan scoffed. He waved his pass again and the light above turned green and stayed that way, allowing Rina to enter her ward.

She'd only managed to take a few steps before a patient of hers came up to her. "Dr. Thennley," she said shyly.

"Morning, Jenny," Rina said with a soft smile. "It's Dr. Kent now, though. I'm sure it will be hard for many, especially me, to get used to that."

Jenny lowered her head. "I had a bit of a hard weekend. Can we talk?"

"I'm sorry to hear, Jenny. Let's talk. Can I get settled in first, though? I'll come right back and find you. Okay?"

Jenny nodded. "Okay."

Rina thanked her and headed towards the main rec area. Patients were lined up taking their medicine from Nurse Bethany Myder. Already she could hear the coarse voice of the nurse demanding some of the patients who didn't require morning meds to step out of the line.

Sometimes Rina thought of Bethany as the sheriff of the ward, instead of a psychiatric nurse. She had voiced her concerns to the Chief of Psychiatry, Dr. Greber, but he said he wasn't able to do much about her. Her union protected her, even though she had managed to give the wrong medications to several patients in the past six months, in addition to her abusive tone with the patients.

Rina looked past her to the large windows. She always enjoyed taking in the view from the rec room that faced the dense woods beyond the parking lot. She enjoyed bird watching from here with some patients. It was a calming activity, looking out into forest.

Nurse Bethany barked at a patient, "Stop it, Edward. You know I need to see you take the pills! Now, open your mouth." The patient was new to the ward this week. He had been sectioned by police after attacking his neighbor for thinking he was an alien. Schizophrenia was such a difficult diagnosis to work with at first and required a lot of building trust with a patient for better results.

"Good morning, Edward," Rina said, interjecting. "How are you?"

Edward smiled. "Morning, Dr. The— or Dr. Kent, now, right?"

"Great memory, Ed. Is everything okay with your new meds?"

"I was just making sure he took his pills, Dr. Kent," Nurse Bethany said sternly.

"Thanks, Bethany." Rina didn't look at her. If she had, she wouldn't have been able to hide her disgust for the woman at that moment. "Are you having any bad side effects?"

"I haven't been sleeping," Ed said, rubbing the side of his head. "The meds are making it impossible."

Rina nodded. "Let's chat really quick before I leave. I can lessen the dose. Figuring out the best medications can be difficult but once we do you will feel so much better."

"Thanks, Doc," Ed said. "Do I need to take these, then?"

"How about you give those back to Bethany, and when we meet in my office, we can fix your meds?"

Ed thanked her again and went across the rec room to grab a puzzle from the shelf. Rina noticed her colleagues, Dr. Sarah Alloy and Dr. Adam Greber, talking to each other. Dr. Greber was in his last month as the chief psychiatrist at Holy Saints hospital.

It was said that either Rina or Dr. Alloy would be up for the promotion after Dr. Greber retired. The only fault Rina thought she had was her tardiness. If she were to self-evaluate she thought she was better at connecting with patients, building strong rapports with them that helped with their recovery. Dr. Alloy had been a psychiatrist at Holy Saints for over five years. She had been biding her time for this promotion.

Even though Rina had only been on staff for the past year, she knew she had the edge on her colleague. She could only imagine the frustration Sarah felt.

"Next!" Nurse Bethany called, and another patient came up to her.

Rina looked at a small foldable table that had some pamphlets on it. She shook her head. It was the only furniture in the room not stuck to the ground, which wasn't protocol.

"We should probably put these pamphlets somewhere else," she said to Bethany.

"Talk to Dr. Alloy," Bethany barked back. "She put the

table here. It's not my job to move it."

Rina sighed. She picked up a pamphlet. It was about a new outpatient program that Sarah was running for patients after they were discharged. The printed sheet had only Dr. Alloy's name on it, not Rina's even though it was Rina's idea to have stronger outpatient support. She had brought it up in conversation with Sarah about a week ago, and her colleague had disregarded it, suggesting their caseloads were already heavy enough and there was no financing for additional staff.

Rina looked back at Sarah Alloy talking to the soon to be retired Dr. Greber. It was obvious what Sarah was doing. She wanted to show her initiative. Sure, it annoyed her that Sarah would put only her name on the program's information, but what made Rina really upset was the table itself. There was a reason why no furniture could be movable, and everything was secured to the floor. It was for the patients' safety.

Part of Rina wanted to interrupt their conversation to tell Sarah about the safety hazard she made in the ward in front of Dr. Greber. Rina reminded herself that she was leaving on her honeymoon today. She didn't want bad blood between her and Sarah. After all, no matter who got the promotion, they would still be working with each other. She would be sure to tell Sarah about her concerns in private.

In her peripheral vision she spotted Jenny Berange, her head down, in the corner of the room. Rina had seen her this way before when she was first admitted to Holy Saints. She had been brought to the ward after police talked her down from jumping off a bridge into the Bow River. The first few days at the unit, Jenny would stand in the corner beside the window for hours at a time, not wanting to talk to anyone.

Rina had worked tirelessly on finding a connection with her. She was only nineteen. A pretty young girl, with so much potential ahead of her if she could get her mental health in line. Being her assigned psychiatrist, Rina had read her file, of course. She knew the abuse she took from her father. She knew the neglect her mother had for her. She had been diagnosed with acute psychosis and feared that unknown forces were after her.

When no progress was being made with Jenny, many had assumed she would be discharged and attempt to kill herself again. Rina had continued to work on finding a connection with the young woman. One morning she observed that Jenny was reading an Agatha Christie novel while standing in the corner. Rina brought similar books from her home library for Jenny and would put them on a table near where she stood. Eventually, Jenny started to read them. Then Rina would spend clinical time reading with her and discussing their favourite parts of the stories. It was almost as if they had started a book club for the two of them. Within a week she was a different person to the distraught girl escorted to the ward.

Now, Rina looked at Jenny standing in the corner of the room as if it were her first day again at Holy Saints. She took a deep breath. Mental health could be very circular in nature. You get better, then worse. Many people who struggled were never a hundred percent better in the end, but hopefully had more tools for taking better care of themselves by the time they left the ward. Whenever her patients were at a low point, all Rina could do was help them with medicine and techniques for handling their symptoms.

Rina was about to ask Jenny to chat in her office when she saw Sarah and Dr. Greber walk towards her, and she put the pamphlet back down on the table.

"Morning, Dr. Kent," Dr Greber said. "That was a fun wedding. I'm surprised we don't have too many hungover doctors and nurses around this morning."

Rina laughed. "Well, they had Sunday to recover."

"Congratulations, Rina," Sarah said. "So, you're only working a little today, right? When's your flight?"

Rina was annoyed at the mention of her reduced hours so she could leave on her honeymoon but smiled. "In seven hours."

Dr. Greber interjected. "We need to have a quick meeting."

"No problem," Rina said.

The three of them walked down the hall to Dr. Greber's

office. He shut the door behind him. "We should do our roundtable review of our patients before you leave."

Rina sometimes hated these reviews. It was important for them to discuss patients and their recoveries. Dr. Greber would add his input when needed, but mostly let Sarah and Rina do what they felt was required. He was a good boss in that way, she thought. He didn't micromanage people or their personalities. He trusted his staff and knew when he needed to be involved.

Rina hoped that someday she would be as good of a chief psychiatrist as Adam Greber, if she got the job. Interviews would be starting in a month.

After an hour of reviewing patients, Dr. Greber mentioned Jenny's case.

"Great work with Jenny," he said. "Truly amazing how she opened up to you. It's remarkable how you've developed the rapport you have with her in such a short time. You brought home some of your charts for her case file. I wanted to look at them with a special group I'm a part of where we review rapport development with patients. I was hoping to use Jenny's case as a prime example of how to do it well."

Rina smiled. "Thanks, Adam." She tutted. "I forgot them in the car though. I'll run out right now."

"Those are confidential reports, Rina," Sarah said with a tone. "Try not to forget them in your vehicle."

"It's a simple mistake, Sarah," Adam replied. He looked at Rina. "Please grab them, though."

Rina stood up from the couch and nodded to Sarah before leaving the office. She had to bite her tongue at how annoyed she was at her colleague, who was obviously attempting to make her look bad. Rina immediately went down the hall, passing the rec room again.

Jenny wasn't in the corner. She was by the foldable table, looking at the pamphlet.

Rina walked up to her. "Is that program something you would be interested in, Jenny? It's not just Dr. Alloy doing it, but me too. I would love to see you even after your time in Holy

Saints."

Jenny put the pamphlet down, lowering her head.

"Jenny?" Rina asked. "I need to go to the parking lot to grab something. Can you wait by my office? I'll be right there, and we can talk. Please."

Jenny raised her head. "They have no eyes," she said in a whisper, "but they see... They have no ears, but they hear – everything."

Rina took a deep breath. She hadn't heard Jenny talk this way for some time. She knew whatever set her off this weekend would be a big blow to her progress. A change in medications would certainly need to be considered.

"Jenny," she said, touching her shoulder gently, "please wait by my office. I'll be right there."

Jenny took a few steps in that direction. "Okay, Dr. Kent."

Rina watched her patient slowly walk away, feeling saddened for the young girl. She had been talking to a social worker about emergency housing for Jenny. Her parents wanted her to return home with them, but given the details in her file, Rina worried about the environment she would be returning to.

Sarah and Adam left the office down the hall and she snapped out of it. She hurried past Ryan, the security guard, down the stairs and back into the parking lot. She ran to her car and opened the door, looking around the nearly empty vehicle to find only a few Starbucks coffee cups, half drunk, in the cup holders.

She panicked, thinking of the conversation she would have with Dr. Greber and Sarah. "Oh – I only misplaced Jenny Berange's file. No big deal, right?" Sarah Alloy was already on a roll today, throwing Rina under the bus any time she could to make herself look better.

She tried to think back to what she did with the file after she left work yesterday. She vividly remembered taking the file from her office and leaving the ward with it. She remembered getting into Jonas's car and him making a comment about taking work home with her again.

Of course, she'd left it in Jonas's car. They drove to work together that day since they had the same shift. She locked her car and ran across the parking lot to her husband's car. She peeked through the back passenger window and sitting neatly on the black leather seating was the file.

Now she would have to get the keys from Jonas and get the file at light speed. She could already imagine the things Sarah would be saying to Adam Greber if she didn't promptly return.

"Rina's a fine psychiatrist – but unorganized. You need someone who will be here on time, and ready for her day. When you retire, don't you want someone to carry on your legacy in a decent way?"

She could almost see Sarah's smile as she delivered her speech. Happy that she didn't have to do anything besides let Rina be Rina to get the promotion.

A loud crash above her made Rina look up. Large pieces of glass fell around her. Rina covered her eyes but felt a shard cut her forearm and winced in pain.

Something heavy bounced off Jonas's car, and there was a deep thud on the concrete in front of her.

When she removed her hand from her eyes, the disfigured body of Jenny lay in front of her. Her limbs, now pointing at unnatural angles, convulsed, reaching out. Within moments, she stopped moving.

Rina turned away and found the table from the rec room had landed on Jonas's car. Pamphlets for Sarah's outpatient program were scattered across the roof and surrounding area. Pieces of glass continued to sprinkle from the fourth-floor window. Rina covered her mouth to muffle her screams.

She stopped as she felt the pain in her arm. Blood was running from the large gash on it.

"Are you okay?" she heard a voice call out, but Rina didn't address them. Instead, she looked one last time at her patient, Jenny.

CHAPTER 2

Six months later.

Dr. Adam Gerber sat at his dining table, the intruder in his home sitting across from him. He took a sip of the fresh orange juice his wife made that day. As he did, his hand shook uncontrollably, spilling it over his suit jacket.

Adam tried not to look at the intruder's face, even though it was covered with a black ski mask. He especially tried not to look at the intruder's handgun, which was aimed directly at his chest. Adam trembled as he put the cup of juice back on the table and took a bite of his biscuit. There was something calming in doing something normal during something chaotic.

The masked intruder had entered his home right after his wife, Vanessa, left to go to their son's for the day to babysit his grandson. The intruder didn't even have to break in, since the door wasn't locked. Nobody in the small town of Carrington, Alberta, locked their doors. Vanessa was not so trusting. She'd grown up in the larger city of Calgary, where crime was more commonplace. She would remind Adam several times a week to lock the doors, but Adam Greber had never been used to the practise. He tried not to imagine his wife saying, "I told you so, Adam."

"You can... take whatever you want," Adam said, his voice trembling as much as his hands. When the Intruder didn't respond, he lowered his head. "I have... money. I have a lot of money."

"Are you finished?" the intruder asked. Adam looked at them now. The thought of being robbed scared him so he couldn't think straight, but the voice of his intruder knocked him out of his daze. He knew exactly who it was. The intruder took off their ski mask, confirming their identity.

"Why?" Adam asked. "Why now?"

"You know why," the intruder said with a smile.

"The girl?" Adam answered. "It's about the girl, isn't it?"

This time the intruder didn't verbally respond but raised the gun at Adam's head.

"No!" he pleaded. "Wait! I did nothing wrong! I promised. We promised we wouldn't hurt her! She will be fine!"

"Are you finished with your... snack?" the intruder asked again.

Adam took a quick sip of his wife's juice. "I... I have kids, you know. Grandkids!"

The intruder smiled. "I know, Adam. I know."

Adam put his head down. "What I'm saying is, I wouldn't hurt that girl, because I'm a father myself."

"I think you're finished now," the intruder said, standing from their chair, and raising the gun. "You should have done something better with your retirement than what you did! Now you pay for your sins."

"But!" Adam shouted. "You don't have to—"

He saw the muzzle flash, followed by a push on his chest. He fell backwards, landing on his kitchen floor. He looked up and saw his blood staining his white kitchen backsplash. He turned to his side, screaming. Sliding his body across the tiled floor, leaving a trail of his life's blood like a snail behind him.

The intruder stepped in front of him.

"No!" Adam cried out. He looked up at the intruder one last time. He raised his arm towards them in a plea, but they kicked his hand with their boot.

The intruder smiled. "I know you won't hurt her – now."

Adam heard the click of the intruder's gun, and then nothing at all.

CHAPTER 3

Rina Kent parked in her usual spot at Holy Saints. She was nearly two hours early. She walked through the lot, noticing Jonas's car in his regular space. She covered her head with her hand in a poor attempt to slow the rain from drenching her. The rainfall had been extreme in the past week to the point that local beaches were closed due to high water and stronger currents. Some areas of Carrington were temporarily closed due to flood damage and the formation of large puddles in the streets.

Rina gazed up at the fourth-floor window of the psych ward, rain striking her face forcefully. Rina hated passing the spot where it happened, but there was no other way for employees to get to the building.

Besides, *everything* was repaired now. Everything was back to how it was supposed to be. Jonas's car was fixed, as if nothing had happened. The rec room window was replaced. The ward had patients check in and check out, as usual.

Everything around Rina had gone back to normal. Rina looked down at her ringless finger. Everything had gone back to… almost normal.

She quickly made her way into the hospital, and up to the fourth floor. She passed Ryan the security guard without a word. He opened the door after a few swipes of his pass, admitting her inside.

She walked past the rec room, where Nurse Bethany was already reminding patients that it would be time for them to go to their rooms for the night soon. As always, everything the nurse said reminded her more of an order.

"Lights out soon!" she barked. The patients largely ignored her, resuming their activities as if nothing had been said. Most of them knew the routine without her forceful prompts.

Bethany gave Rina an ugly smile. "Early for your night shift, Dr. Thennley."

Nurse Bethany had been starting to call Rina by her maiden name, even though she hadn't officially changed it. Even though Rina had reminded her that it was still "Dr. Kent", she continued to make the mistake.

"Everything okay tonight?" Rina asked.

Bethany nodded. She rubbed her eyes, smudging some of her dark blue eyeshadow. "All fine. Are you only working nights at the hospital now?"

Rina took a deep breath. The psychiatrists took turns doing the overnight rotations. Lately she had been opting to only work midnights and had requested to Dr. Alloy, now the Chief of Psychiatry, that she do so permanently. She could see no reason why Sarah would deny this to her. Rina still kept hours during the daytime for clinical work with her assigned patients but she was available for the entire hospital during her midnight shifts.

Rina knew firsthand the struggles of shift work. It would be better for the psychiatrists at Holy Saints to have a permanent night psychiatrist. Consistent workdays were a positive change that could benefit everyone. She would ask Sarah for an update on her request soon.

Since she'd been awarded the promotion after Dr. Greber retired the month before, Rina had to admit that her new boss was doing a great job. Things were running smoothly in the ward, and in the hospital. All psychiatric care needs were met.

Midnights were best for Rina. She barely slept through the night anyway. She had better luck napping in the day. Besides, it was easier to avoid her ex-husband at night. He rarely worked midnights in his rotation. Seeing him less made things… a little easier.

"I'm going for my workout," Rina said, ignoring Bethany's question. "If you need me, you can find me at the gym."

Bethany smiled. "I won't need you. Dr. Alloy and Dr. Knowles are still here."

Dr. Belinda Knowles was recently hired as Holy Saints new psychiatrist on the ward after Sarah was promoted. Rina was surprised to hear that. Typically, Dr. Knowles would switch with Rina between morning and night shifts. Sarah, though, would typically be gone before Rina started.

"Why are they here?" she asked.

Bethany looked over her shoulder towards a conference room. "A new girl was admitted today. They have both been talking to her for some time."

Rina glanced at the closed conference room. They typically did the intake process there. What was surprising was that Sarah was taking part in the meeting as well. Why would both her and Belinda be there?

Walking past the conference room was Cody Alder, a psychiatric nurse on ward. Cody was much younger than Rina. She placed him around twenty-two or twenty-three. She'd never bothered to ask because the slightest attention you gave the boy would be perceived as flirty.

The nurses on ward worked a similar rotation schedule to psychiatrists but lately Cody had been opting to work more midnight shifts, with Rina. When he spotted her looking in his direction, he smiled and sauntered up to her and Bethany.

"Evening, Doctor," he said with a smirk. Bethany rolled her eyes and left the conversation, giving some type of command to a nearby patient.

"Hey, Cody," Rina said curtly. "How's the ward tonight?"

"I've been doing great," Cody said, seemingly misunderstanding her question. "Midnights have been killing me lately, though. I don't know why you like them so much."

Rina shrugged in response.

"When are you taking your break tonight?"

She gave a thin smile. "You know me – I don't have breaks."

"Always in your office, reviewing files, or whatever else you do in there."

"Just working," Rina said, annoyed.

"Well, if you're up for an actual break, let me know. I'll bring coffee to your office for us."

"Thanks," Rina said, "but I'll be okay. I'm early for my shift and wanted to get a workout in. I'll be in the gym if anybody needs me."

"I'll come find you then," Cody said, smiling. "Have a good workout."

Rina left the ward with her gym bag that she kept in her office, passing Ryan without saying a word. She went to the changing room across the hall from the gym. Holy Saints gym was… small. It was mostly used by staff, but sometimes by patients when supervised.

She changed into her sports bra, slipping on her loose workout shirt. Six months ago, her workout shirts were nearly skin-tight. Almost everything in her wardrobe was oversized now. Rina estimated that she'd lost nearly twenty-five pounds over the last few months. She wished she had kept track of what her starting weight was better, but she assumed she started around a hundred and twenty-three pounds. With her being only five-foot, six inches, she knew it gave her an almost malnourished appearance. She felt she took adequate care of herself, though, and would try not to take it personally when she noticed people gazing at her slender figure.

The truth was Rina loved to run now, especially before and sometimes after her shift. It helped clear her mind. It helped her stay centered. She knew how she looked, though, and knew she needed to eat more now that she was using more energy.

Rina walked across the hall, a white towel swung over her shoulder, and into the gym. The room only had two treadmills, an elliptical, and resistance bands. The gym used to have heavy dumbbells, but a patient dropped one, hurting his foot, and management decided to remove them. Now the room only had a set of five-pound weights and different resistance bands.

She didn't care much for weights anyway. She only enjoyed running. She stepped onto a machine and hit the quick start button. She stared at the white brick wall the machine faced as it started to move.

She quickly raised the incline by a few levels and pushed the pace up until she was at a light jog.

A new girl was coming to the ward, Bethany had said. She remembered Bethany's ugly smile that grew after she mentioned it. Why did Bethany smile that way?

How old was the girl? Rina immediately thought of Jenny. Instead of letting her thoughts run, she increased her speed. She started to breathe heavily and could feel her body heating.

She thought of Jonas and the day Jenny killed herself. Rina and Jonas didn't make their flight for their honeymoon that day. They never rescheduled it either. Rina only worked. Jonas worked. They had other patients to tend to, Rina knew. She couldn't just leave them, go on a vacation. She and Jonas could have their honeymoon when it was more appropriate, she'd thought.

They never had their honeymoon.

She wasn't sure when Jonas started to hate her, but Rina knew the day their marriage was over. Jonas wanted to try marriage counselling but that wasn't an option for Rina. She didn't need counselling. She didn't need help.

Jonas had even pushed to move across the country, and sometimes overseas. At times he suggested working in entirely different occupations as well. Rina had thought he was the lunatic. The amount of student debt they had incurred educating themselves in their chosen occupations was enough to terrify anybody.

Rina didn't need to find a new place to live, or a new job, or counselling. Afterall, it was Jonas who broke their vow, not her. Jonas was the one who went behind her back.

Why did Rina need counseling?

She raised the speed on the treadmill and was now full-out sprinting.

The lights in the room flickered, but she paid no attention to them. For a moment the lights turned off for several seconds. Rina panicked and was about to jump off the machine when they came back on.

Rina sighed as she maintained her speed. What an old junk hospital. She was excited to start working at the new one. Sarah had told her there would be a larger gym there. But construction was going slower than expected. The grand opening had been delayed an additional year. Some wondered if it would ever open. Anytime Rina drove by the construction area, she never saw anybody working. She wondered when crews were on site, or if they even existed.

The new hospital would be a new start for her. It would be larger. More staff. Jonas would be there of course, but she would see him less.

She pushed the speed up an additional level and tried to not think about the pain. She could feel her body breaking down under the pressure and enjoyed pushing herself.

Suddenly the lights turned off completely, and the treadmill stopped working. Rina ran into the front of the treadmill, taking a blow to her shoulder.

She winced in pain as she stepped off. The small gym had no windows, and somehow, no emergency lighting. The door creaked open, and Rina saw the dim light from the red emergency lights in the hallway outside, and a large, shadowy figure in the doorway. Rina waited for them to say something, but the person remained still, not moving.

"Hello," she called out.

The figure moved its arm and turned on a flashlight, beaming it at Rina. She covered her face until they moved it away.

"There you are," Ryan the security guard said. "So dark in here."

"Breaker is out again?"

"The maintenance guy is on it. Dr. Alloy asked me to get you. She wants you to come to her office right away."

CHAPTER 4

Rina followed Ryan to Sarah's office. She wondered why the security guard was leading her to her boss's office when she clearly knew where it was. Ryan stayed several paces ahead of her, occasionally looking back to ensure Rina was still following.

As they walked through the ward, most of the patients were heading to their bedrooms for the night, except a young brunette girl sitting at a small table by herself with a pile of puzzle pieces grouped on one side. She assembled the pieces quickly, rocking back and forth in her chair. Many patients enjoyed putting together puzzles, but Rina couldn't tell if the girl did. The girl's eyes widened, exposing the whites, as she worked on the puzzle. She didn't appear to be blinking as far as Rina could tell. She held a thin blue notebook under her armpit as she put pieces together.

For a moment she thought of Jenny Berange. She was young and a brunette just like this girl, only Jenny would never sit at a table. She would always stand in the corner, observing everything around her, questioning its threat level. This new patient, though, was intensely observant of her puzzle but likely nothing else, it seemed.

Rina looked at the large window in the rec room. The glass may have been replaced, but she couldn't forget what happened. Rina touched her forearm, feeling the area where the wound from the shard had been. It had healed well but left a dark scar on her arm.

Ryan led her down the hall, towards the office. Rina

looked back again at the girl. Nurse Bethany had walked over to her at the table.

"It's nighttime, hon," she said with her hoarse voice. "Time to put the puzzle away. I told you not to take out a puzzle so close to lights out. Put it away and you can put it together when you have time tomorrow."

The girl continued to put her puzzle pieces together, not paying attention to the nurse. After a few moments, Bethany grabbed the puzzle box and slid her hand across the table, sweeping each piece into the box as they fell.

Ryan turned his head, confirming Rina was still with him as they got closer to Sarah's office, which unsettled Rina. Why did security need to escort her to her boss's office? Was she about to be fired, she wondered. Impossible. Why would they fire her? She had done nothing for the last six months but commit herself to the ward and her patients. She had given everything she had to them. She had *nothing* else in her life besides her work.

She breathed a sigh of relief when Ryan opened Sarah's office door, and she and Dr. Knowles were sitting and laughing.

"Hey," Sarah said. She nodded at Ryan, thanking him for finding Rina, and he left, closing the door behind him. "Sorry to bug you before your shift. I was hoping you were here early today."

"Is everything okay?" Rina asked. "Is it one of my patients?"

Sarah looked at her with concern for a moment, before smiling again. "No, but we've had an interesting intake today with a young woman."

"I think I saw her in the rec area," Rina said, intrigued now.

"It's Dr. Deaver's niece," Belinda said.

Rina raised an eyebrow and looked at Sarah. "I had no clue Phyllis had a niece."

Sarah nodded. "Yeah, and thankfully she's nothing like Phyllis Deaver." She laughed at her own joke. Belinda smiled but Rina waited for her to continue. Everybody at Holy Saints hospital knew Dr. Phyllis Deaver was a... bitch, for lack of a better description. She had been the hospital's only pediatrician on staff for the past ten years. You would assume that someone who wanted to work with children's healthcare would have a special calling for it, would be warm and fuzzy, would have an empathetic aura, but not Phyllis.

"I didn't even know Phyllis had a sister, for that matter," Belinda said. "I assumed the devil was her father, though." Belinda laughed at her own joke as well, but this time Sarah didn't react.

"Phyllis Deaver's sister, Marie, is actually missing," Sarah said. "She's been missing for over a month now. Phyllis likes to keep that to herself as much as possible but most management knows about her situation. She took a few weeks off when Marie left. I'm only telling you two now because, well, her daughter, Phyllis's niece, has been admitted to Holy Saints."

"Why was she admitted?" Rina asked. "Was it due to her mother's disappearance?"

Sarah nodded. "I'm sure it has something to do with her being here, but the main reason is because she tried to... kill herself. She tried to overdose on Tylenol. She was in the ER most of yesterday and today." Sarah looked at Rina. "Jonas was her doctor in the ER, you should know. Thankfully she was alright, and now that she's stable physically, she's been admitted to our ward."

"What's her name?"

Sarah laughed. "What a night; I completely forgot that part. Amy. Amy Deaver."

"Does she have any cognitive issues because of the Tylenol overdose?" Rina asked.

"None that we can identify. She has autism. Talking to Phyllis, she's been non-verbal for years. Which makes this case even harder. Belinda and I tried to do our intake process together with Amy, but no luck. She didn't answer a word. She stared off into the room, ignoring us completely."

Belinda shook her head. "People with autism have a

higher chance of suicide, too. This is going to be a hard case."

Sarah nodded. "That's right. Our job, though, is just to help stabilize her enough so she can leave Holy Saints with some type of safety plan. With how the young woman is, I'm not sure what change we can make besides her environment when she's discharged."

"Okay," Belinda said.

Sarah looked at Rina and then back at Belinda. "I know times are busy. All of us have too many patients on our caseload. We barely have enough time to give to any of them. Amy is an eighteen-year-old girl, who's suicidal, autistic, and doesn't speak. Worse, Phyllis Deaver is going to be breathing down our necks on this since she's her aunt. I don't want her around our ward, but we know she's going to be a presence while Amy is with us. This is a tough patient to work with. I don't want to add stress to anybody's caseload intentionally. Do I have a volunteer to take her on?"

Sarah again looked at Rina, but she didn't respond. Instead, Rina pretended to be deep in thought, as if questioning if she should take Amy on, even though she already knew the answer.

Belinda broke the silence. "I can take her."

Sarah smiled. "Thanks Belinda. I owe you on this one. Tag me in anytime you need help. I'll try to mitigate the Phyllis Deaver problem."

"Well, now it will be easy," Belinda said with a laugh.

"Thank you both for coming to see me," Sarah said. "Sorry to take you away from your workout, Rina."

"No problem, Dr. Alloy," Rina said. Rina lowered her head. She tried her best, but could only think of Jenny Berange, standing in the corner of the rec room before jumping through the broken window. She couldn't get the final image of her patient out of her mind.

Rina felt her eyes start to water. She quickly turned her face to hide it from her colleagues. She opened Sarah's door, and Belinda stood up.

"Oh, Rina," Sarah said with a smile, "one last thing I was hoping to talk to you about. Can you stay?"

Rina nodded, quickly wiping her eyes. Belinda smiled at her as she left the office. Rina closed the door and stood in the corner, looking back at Sarah.

Sarah gestured for her to sit, and Rina complied.

"I'm worried about you," Sarah said. "You've been working these midnight shifts, continuously taking them from me and Belinda. I hate midnights too, but I worry about you taking all of them. It's summertime and it's been really helpful, though. I don't want to put you down for offering that to me and Belinda."

"It's no problem, Sarah," Rina said. "I like midnight, to be honest. We talked about the potential of me doing it on a full-time basis, and I wanted to follow up with you on that."

Sarah sighed. "I… don't think it's a good time right now."

Rina lowered her head, trying to hide her frustration. "Why?" she asked sternly. "It would benefit you and Belinda not to work them. You guys could give more to your patients if you're not dead tired from working a shift rotation. I mean… you're the Chief of Psychiatry! You shouldn't have to work them. I can handle overnights. I can still work with my patients during my clinical time in the evenings or mornings before I leave."

Sarah sighed again. "Why didn't you take Amy Deaver?"

Rina raised an eyebrow. "Like you said, it's busy. I'm thinking about my own self-care."

"Self-care," Sarah repeated. "You basically live in the hospital these days."

"I want to be available for my patients."

Sarah nodded. "I'm not doubting your intentions."

"Then what are you doubting?"

Sarah stood up from her desk, taking in a deep breath. "Before, you would have taken Amy Deaver's case in a microsecond. Is it because of what happened to Jenny Berange?"

"My caseload is busy," Rina said, ignoring the question. "Like you said, it's a busy time. That's it."

"Your caseload," Sarah repeated. "That's another thing."

"What about my caseload?"

Sarah sat again. "We all love a nice, easy patient on our caseload. A few cases of functional depression. Suicidal ideation, with no actual plan to harm themselves. A treatable food disorder. Your caseload... is full of them."

Rina stood up. "How dare you. I give everything to this hospital. If that's not enough for you, then fire me. I won't sit here and take this from you."

"I never wanted to say this to you," Sarah said, nodding her head. "It should have been you, okay."

"What are you talking about?"

"You should have gotten my position. Everybody knew it was going to be you." Sarah stood up, went over to her PhD diploma that hung on the wall, and moved it until it seemed more level. "If it wasn't for what happened with Jenny, it would have been you." She looked back at Rina, taking in a deep breath.

"You worked hard to get this role, Sarah." Rina lowered her head. "And since we're sharing, I guess I can tell you you've been a good boss."

"That means a lot, but still... I worry about you. Maybe you should take some time off."

Rina shook her head. "No, I don't need time off. Work helps me, to be honest. Keeps me busy."

"You would do anything for your patients, right?"

"Of course," Rina said instantly.

"Take some time off," Sarah repeated. "You can't give them anymore when you're at your limit. When you come back, you'll be refreshed, and ready to give them everything, but with a full tank."

Rina smiled and shook her head. "And what happens with my patients?"

Sarah sat at her desk again. "We can figure something out that's temporary."

"The caseloads are too high for you and Belinda to take them on, even if they are the *easy* ones. So, I guess that means a new psychiatrist coming to the ward? Will someone replace me?"

"Just temporarily," Sarah repeated.

Rina laughed out loud. "You just want to replace me, don't you? Well, thanks, Dr. Alloy, for this one-on-one, ..." Rina tilted her head. "Did you speak with Adam about me?"

"Adam Greber?" Sarah said, surprised. "No, I haven't seen him in a long time." When Rina didn't respond, she continued, "I heard about the incident at his retirement party with you and him, but I didn't get involved and I never spoke to him about you or my concerns, okay?"

"Okay," Rina repeated, turning to leave.

"Rina," Sarah called out, but she had already opened the office door and stormed out.

CHAPTER 5

Rina attempted to leave the ward without acknowledging anyone. Most of the patients were already inside their rooms for the night. When she walked past the rec area, though, Amy was still sitting at the desk like before, quietly humming a song.

Rina stopped and watched her for a moment. She wondered how Belinda would reach this girl. She was completely in her own world. Nothing else mattered. Even Nurse Bethany couldn't get her to go to her room for the night.

Rina jumped when Cody appeared beside her. His shoulder nudged hers. "Anytime she grabs a new puzzle, Bethany takes it away," he said. "We decided to let her acclimate more to the ward before reminding her to go to her room. Hopefully, by the time everyone else is in their rooms, we can get her to go to hers. Or maybe you could talk to her?"

Rina lowered her head. "I haven't started work yet. I still have some time before my shift." She started to walk off when Cody reached out and gently touched her arm.

"Where are you going?" he asked.

Rina shrugged him off, unable to hold her frustration with him touching her. She leaned in closer. "Please – don't touch me like that again. I'll be back when my shift starts."

Cody shrugged innocently. "Sheesh, I wasn't touching you inappropriately. I was trying to get your attention. Don't bite my head off, Rina."

"Dr. Kent," she said sternly.

He rolled his eyes. "Fine, Dr. Kent. I'll see you soon – when your shift starts."

Rina bit her tongue, holding back what she really wanted to say to the boyish nurse. Instead, she continued down the hall, and out the ward doors. She went to the elevator and let out a loud sigh when she remembered it was out of order. She clenched her teeth, trying not to scream with frustration as she headed to the stairway.

Who did Sarah Alloy think she was, talking to her the way she had? To make statements about her caseload being *easy*? Rina wondered what she would say to Sarah if she didn't fear losing her job. She smiled, thinking about the different cuss words she could utilize to make Sarah's face even more pale than it already was.

When she opened the stairway door, she heard footsteps coming up. Rina almost sighed audibly when she saw it was Phyllis Deaver.

"Good," Phyllis said, storming up the stairs. "I was just about to find you." She was over forty, and single. She maintained an average figure, with an average fairness to her appearance, but had an intense aura to her that appeared to repel most men. Rina couldn't remember ever seeing her with a man in a romantic way.

"My shift starts in an hour, Phyllis," she said. "Can we chat then?"

Phyllis shook her head. "It's been a long night for me. With what happened with Amy, and we had a lot of kids in the ER. Dr. Kent— I mean, Jonas helped where he could but I'm exhausted. I wanted to check in with staff about Amy. How's she doing so far?"

Rina shrugged. "Well, Belinda's been assigned to work with her. You should check with—"

"Belinda?" Phyllis scoffed. "I thought for sure you would have had her."

"Sorry," Rina said, "but Belinda I'm sure would love to give you an update. I think she left for the day, though."

"Well, she's gone, and you're here. Why can't you give me

an update? Didn't you meet her yet? Amy?"

"No, but from what I understand, she isn't talking to anybody."

Phyllis laughed. "She's never talked to me either. Marie, my sister, they had something special. My sister said Amy would speak at times. Now that she's— well, I'm sure you know."

Rina had felt aggravated by Phyllis's presence when all she wanted was to get out of the hospital until her shift started, but as soon as she mentioned her sister, she felt empathy.

"My sister," Phyllis said, taking her time. "Amy was homeschooled. Marie did her best to help Amy learn, but her disability made that difficult. Now... her daughter is here. And you... don't seemingly care."

Rina took a deep breath. "You know that's not true. We all want to make sure Amy will be okay when she leaves here. Hopefully, Amy can grieve for your sister not being there."

"She's not dead, my sister, at least I think so – the police do too. They closed her missing persons case. She left a note in her room. She asked to not be found. She hoped I would care for Amy." When she said her niece's name, she lowered her head. "I think about how my sister just left, leaving Amy. All Amy had was my sister. That's it. Amy used to talk, but only to Marie. To think of everything I did for Marie!" Phyllis said, raising her voice. "And... she just leaves, left me Amy with me. Now... Amy's here and..."

Phyllis couldn't say the words, but Rina knew full well what she meant. She knew exactly what she was going through.

Guilt.

Amy had attempted to hurt herself, and Phyllis Deaver, despite her coldness, felt the guilt of her niece's actions.

"This isn't your fault," Rina said, placing a hand on her shoulder. "It isn't."

"My fucking sister," Phyllis said. "I need you to help Amy, please. I know you're not her assigned psychiatrist. Belinda is useless, you know that, and I do too. I know what you can do, Rina."

"Just talk to Belinda. She's great, really."

"It's because of that girl, what was her name? Last year, the one who killed herself. I hear her name around the hospital still. That's why you won't see Amy, isn't it?"

"Phyllis," Rina said sternly. "Talk to Belinda about it."

"You just told me it wasn't my fault, Rina," Phyllis said. Rina looked down and saw Deaver was clenching her fist. "If it wasn't my fault, it wasn't yours either. Amy needs *good* help."

Rina pushed past Phyllis and entered the stairway. "For fuck's sake, Phyllis, talk to Belinda."

Rina stormed down the stairway, her footsteps echoing in the halls. She opened the door and went into the foyer. Near the exit, blocking her way out, was her ex-husband.

Of course, Rina thought. Whenever I don't want to see him, he magically appears.

Jonas was talking to another ER doctor when he noticed Rina. He shook his colleague's hand and began walking towards her.

Rina tried to maintain herself but didn't know how well she could control her emotions after Sarah and her experience with Phyllis Deaver.

"Hey, Rina," Jonas said with a smile. "How are you?"

"Good," Rina said, not stopping to talk to him.

Jonas tried to keep pace with her. "Listen, I was hoping I could drop by tomorrow and grab some of my stuff I forgot. Would that be okay?"

"Fine, fine," Rina said. "Come whenever." She continued towards the staff exit, and to her disgust, Jonas followed.

"What about you, are you okay?" he asked softly.

Rina stopped and looked back at her ex-husband. "Why would you care?"

Jonas looked around him, as some patients and colleagues took notice of their conversation. "I'm worried, that's all."

"Well everybody's worried about me, it seems. I'm perfectly fine, though."

"Okay," Jonas said. "I... still care for you. I wanted to make sure, that's it. I heard you're working straight midnights now."

Rina shook her head. "From whom? Sarah? Have you been talking to Sarah about your concerns for me? Is that why I had to sit in her office just now and hear it from her?"

Jonas raised his hands in surrender. "Okay, I didn't mean to upset you, and no I didn't talk to Dr. Alloy about you. It's just coming from me, that's it."

"Maybe you should have cared about my feelings before you cheated."

Jonas looked around again, seeing if anybody heard. They were obviously making a scene now. "Can we not do this here? Let's change the subject. How's Denzel doing?"

"I'm trying to leave, Dr. Kent," Rina said with a tone. "Can you let me go now?"

Jonas nodded.

She was finally able to step through the sliding door and into the staff parking lot. It was almost ten at night. She felt relieved when there was nobody in sight outside. There was another hour before shift change for most positions at the hospital. People would start piling into their vehicles after a long day soon, but for now Rina could be by herself.

Jonas's car was parked in the same spot it had been a year ago. In front of his car was the sidewalk where it happened. For most people, it was just a cement path, but for Rina, it was much more. She rolled up her sleeve and touched her scar where the glass cut her.

She walked slowly to the spot where Jenny landed. Rina looked around, and when she was convinced she was alone, she lowered herself, kneeling on the pavement. She touched the cold cement and covered her mouth.

She looked once more around her before beginning to cry.

CHAPTER 6

Rina returned to shift, happy that Belinda and Sarah had already left. Nurse Bethany and Cody stayed on as part of their regular rotation. Rina was also grateful that the young, handsome nurse had seemed to catch the hint that she wasn't interested.

She sat at her desk, thinking of her run-in with Jonas. It upset her that her marriage hadn't lasted a year before falling apart. She reminded herself it was Jonas who ruined everything, not her.

For most people, divorce is never on their mind when they marry, but if Rina was being honest with herself, she thought of the idea a lot on her wedding day. She never wanted to divorce. She never wanted a failed marriage. The last thing she wanted was to be like her parents.

Sometimes Rina thought her father still blamed her for the divorce with her mother. The rational side of Rina knew she wasn't to blame. Despite how her father made her feel, nothing that happened with her parents was Rina's fault. She'd moved across the country to not be reminded of her parents' lonely, separate lives. Both were unhappy.

When Rina was seven her parents divorced. Her father had been quietly meeting with another woman behind her mother's back, and his marriage exploded in his face when Rina's mother started to strongly suspect something. One night, her father dropped her off at her grandmother's house so he could be with his girlfriend. Rina's mother was working a midnight shift as a pharmacy technician at a twenty-four-hour store.

In the morning, when Rina returned home with her father, her mother asked both of them what they had done at Grandma's house. Rina's father said they played board games and watched a movie. When Rina's mother looked at Rina and asked if that's what she had done at Grandma's house, Rina instantly, without thought, said that wasn't true.

"Dad didn't stay at Grandma's house," Rina told her mother that day, laughing. "He picked me up in the morning."

Rina didn't understand why her mom was so upset. She couldn't comprehend why her father seemed just as upset, but only at Rina for answering wrong. Soon after, they divorced. Rina didn't see her father for nearly three years. Her mother would always tell Rina, especially when she was older and started to be more interested in boys, that finding someone who won't leave you when things are tough was what mattered most in marriage. Find someone who never gives up on you, she had told Rina.

When she met Jonas, she thought she had found that man. He was so passionately in love with Rina when they first started dating. Within a year, that passion had developed into a love she never thought possible. She moved to Carrington from Calgary to be closer to him. When he walked towards her at the church on the day of their wedding, all Rina could think was this was a man who loved her and would never leave. Then... he gave up on her.

Rina turned on her work computer and sighed. The night was quiet, as usual. She spent most of it doing what she usually did, creating notes for her patients and re-reading their files. She lined up some clinical time with a few of them in the morning. She hoped she wouldn't have to say anything to Sarah when she saw her.

Rina thought that as the night went her temper would cool, but she only became more upset. She took her lunch break. eating the half-melted granola bar she had grabbed on her way out the door before work, in the workout room after having a run.

Then she changed and quickly went back to the ward. She did a room check on the patients, opening a slot on their doors. The nursing staff had a lot of names they were to look in on hourly, but sometimes Rina would check all of her patients herself to make sure everything was okay.

She stopped at Amy's room, curious. She opened the slot, expecting to see a figure in the dark, rocking, and humming that weird song. She had sung the tune all night before going to her room. The same melody over and over. Instead, she saw the young woman, under the sheets, sleeping.

Rina smiled. She was just a girl, she reminded herself. She was certainly not Jenny Berange either.

"She okay?" Nurse Bethany asked. Rina turned her head and the nurse waited for her reply. "I don't want to open the slot after you."

"She's fine, Bethany," Rina said.

Bethany scribbled something on her clipboard and headed to a different room, opening the slot. Rina closed the one in Amy's door poorly, attempting to avoid making a loud noise but failing miserably. She walked back into her office, and continued to read her patients' files until morning.

A knock on her office door startled her. "Hey," the male nurse said. "Starting morning rounds."

Rina nodded. "Thanks, Cody. Let me know if you need me."

"Are you coming out to greet everyone?" he asked.

"Please, let me know if you need me," she repeated.

"K," Cody said, leaving the office immediately.

Rina eventually went out into the ward, passing some of her patients, reminding them of their appointment times coming up. In the rec room, she found Amy in the same spot as the day before. She sat at the same table, working on a different puzzle. Her notebook was on her lap, tightly guarded.

Amy began to hum her song again. She stopped and glanced around the rec room. Some of the patients were getting in line for the medications, others watching television on the couch together. Most people looked dead tired, but not Amy. The girl's eyes were wide as she connected another piece.

Rina took a chair from a nearby desk and sat on the other side of Amy. The girl didn't acknowledge her and continued to hum her song. It had a rhythm to it Rina recognized. It was almost like something you'd hear young girls sing at a playground.

"Hey, Amy," Rina whispered. "My name is Rina." The girl continued to hum and find another piece from her pile. "Dr. Rina Kent. I'm a psychiatrist." Amy stopped humming a moment, her hand continuing to search in a pile of pieces. When she found the right one, she continued to hum. Rina sighed. What could Belinda do for this girl? She knew in her heart that once the girl was discharged, she would try and do it again, like Belinda suggested happened to many people with autism. Maybe next time she would actually kill herself.

Rina felt her hand tremble. Someone needed to help the girl. Rina... couldn't. Not anymore.

Rina reached out and grabbed Amy's hand firmly. "Please," she said, "don't do it." Rina sighed to herself. "This isn't how we talk to people here." She let go of the girl's hand. "Just... don't kill yourself. Please. I can't— your aunt couldn't handle that. Okay?" The girl continued to ignore Rina, humming her tune.

"What is that song?" Rina asked. "Is it a nursery rhyme?" The girl didn't answer.

"Breakfast!"

She turned and saw Bethany waving for Amy to stand and head towards the cafeteria.

CHAPTER 7

Rina drove home soon after her shift was over. Although it was morning, the cloudy skies lately had made it hard to distinguish night from day. She wasn't used to being back this early from work. Denzel would be happy. Many days she would stay an extra hour or two, unpaid. She wasn't sure if it was her tense conversation with Sarah or the new patient, Amy, which made her want to retreat home. Thankfully, Sarah had not confronted her about their meeting the day before.

When Rina drove down her street she sighed immediately when she saw Jonas's car in the driveway. She parked beside him and got out as Jonas came out of her house with two boxes in his hands. Denzel ran out beside him, licking his hands, wetting the sides of the box.

"Sorry," Jonas said immediately. "I tried knocking first, but nobody was home. I thought after our conversation yesterday it would be better for me to avoid issues by using the key under the mat. I was hoping to grab my stuff before you got home." He laughed awkwardly. "I'm surprised you still keep a key there."

Rina nodded in understanding. She wished he'd been successful in his mission as she didn't need to see him this morning either.

"Very well," she said. "Did you get everything?"

Jonas opened the trunk and placed the boxes in. "Two more." Rina was walking to her front door when Jonas called out to her. "I didn't mean to upset you yesterday, that wasn't my intention."

"I know," she said, not stopping to talk. Denzel barked and followed her.

"You need to know," Jonas said, "I think I'm the biggest idiot alive." Rina stopped in her tracks and turned to her ex-husband.

"What was that?" she asked, confused.

Jonas smiled. "We... go to work every day and try and save people – help people. We became so focused on our work that we forgot to save our marriage. I wish I could have gone back. We could have tried counseling. We could have done... something."

"Sleeping around with a big-boobed nurse wasn't the best treatment option for our marriage," Rina said sternly.

He nodded. "I know. I keep saying this, though, because it's true. I only kissed that nurse at the bar that one time. Nothing else. I haven't talked to her since. She's moved to a different city too. I never pursued her after the mistake I made that night."

"Forgive me for not trusting you, Jonas," she said. "I knew the day I found out, from our colleagues at Holy Saints, that you kissed her. I didn't find out from you, but everyone else. Do you know how embarrassing that was for me? Especially after what happened! I knew that day I couldn't trust again. Listen, it's too early in the morning for us to redo our old arguments."

Jonas raised his hand. "And I get that. I also know the day things went bad for you, which impacted us. The day... *she* died. The day that young woman killed herself."

"It's been a long night, Jonas," Rina said. "I'm tired. Get your boxes, and please leave."

"Okay. I agreed to annul our marriage when you asked. I guess... sometimes I think there's still a chance for us. I want there to still be a chance, Rina. We could do like we talked about. Move. Go somewhere in British Columbia. Enjoy the better weather. We could open small practices and work at a pace we would like. We can work this out. I know we can. I still... I mean, you haven't changed your last name."

"I haven't gotten around to it yet," she said coldly. "I never wanted to move from Carrington. This is my home now. Holy Saints is my home. If you want to move, or have a change, then I wish you all the best... It's busy at work, and changing last names takes time. I will get to it. Now, next time you come, don't use my key, and knock. If I don't answer, knock longer."

Jonas was about to say something when his phone rang. He took out his cell and looked at the screen, picking it up immediately.

"Hey," he said. His face dropped instantly. "What do you mean?" His voice sounded panicked. Jonas was usually cool, even in the highest stress situations. It was part of what made him an excellent ER doctor. His tone was enough for Rina to stop.

"When did this happen?" he asked. "Alright. Thanks for telling me." He ended the call and slipped his cell back into his jeans pocket. He stared at the ground, not moving.

"What's wrong?" Rina asked. "Is everything okay? Was it your father?" She knew his father was having heart troubles. Jonas and his father had a loving relationship. When she was married to him, it ruined Jonas to find out his father had been diagnosed with congestive heart failure.

"No," Jonas said, staring at her. "Thank God, no. That was Caleb Janson. He called to tell me the... news. Adam Greber – he's been murdered."

CHAPTER 8

Adam Greber is dead.

Rina continued to think about him long after Jonas told her. After he left, she immediately put on the television to catch any news clips on it. Being a small town, she assumed it would be plastered on any local station, but it wasn't.

Rina took out her phone and looked up articles on Adam. The first hit in the search was an article talking about him being Chief of Psychiatry at Holy Saints. The picture showed one of him, with Rina and Sarah behind him. She clicked on the link and gawked at the picture. She had read the article before, when it was initially written. It talked about the ward and Adam's work.

She remembered the photographer taking the picture that day. Adam wrapped his arms around the shoulder of Sarah and Rina, but the photographer felt it wasn't professional enough. He asked that Sarah and Rina stand behind Adam, with Dr. Greber folding his arm and smiling at the lens.

Now, Dr. Greber was… murdered. Retired for a little over a month, he had been doing nothing but fishing and spending time with his wife, who was also retired, and his grandchildren.

She clicked back on the search on her phone. Most of the articles were about his work at Holy Saints. Near the bottom of the page was one on him retiring. She clicked on the second page of the search results and found what she was looking for.

"Retired Psychiatrist Found Murdered at His Home", the title read.

She clicked on the short article from a news site she hadn't heard of and read it quickly, but it gave no new information from what she already knew.

Her former mentor had been killed at his home. The police were investigating, and it was confirmed to be murder. The police added a number for anybody with any information.

Rina lay on her couch in shock. Denzel rested beside her, his head in her lap. She thought she would break down in tears after Jonas left, but instead she felt indifferent. She wasn't sad, mad, just... there. She knew her emotions were processing. She knew that she needed more time to understand what had happened, but as she continued with her day she was amazed at her own coldness to the situation.

She mostly liked Adam Greber. She respected his work on the ward. She had hoped she was going to be chosen to take his place. Was that why Rina couldn't find the tears for him? Was she still upset at him for not picking her – or maybe it was how he confronted her at his retirement party. Rina tried not to think about that night. Adam had been intoxicated. The things he said, he didn't mean.

Rina took out a pizza from the freezer and shoved it in the oven. She thought about how her former colleague was murdered as she ate crappy frozen pizza for breakfast. She finished some laundry while thinking that Adam Greber would never do anything meaningless again.

She sat on the couch, staring at the television that was off. She closed her eyes, forcing herself to sleep but failing miserably. Rina wanted to go for a run. Sometimes that would clear her mind enough to think properly.

Her cell rang in her pocket. She leaned to one side to take it out. When she saw it was Sarah Alloy calling, she tossed it along the couch. Rina could barely find her own emotions right now; she didn't want to be buried by someone else's.

She took a deep breath, trying to remember Adam's face. Even though she had seen him nearly every day on the ward, it was as if the memory of what he looked like had faded after she found out about his murder.

She thought about his retirement party. It was at a local pub, Irish bar, Patty O's. It was chosen because it was his favourite place to decompress after a day of working with people and their emotions, much to Rina's surprise. She didn't think Adam was a drinker. He never talked about going to a bar with peers or friends.

It struck her funny how Adam Greber enjoyed talking about his Irish background, and the emotionless culture it had. It could have been the irony that he was a psychiatrist, or shame that he found emotions interesting compared to his ancestors. He talked about that irony at length that night, stuttering his words as he attempted to do so.

Adam drank more than a few pints of ale. He was laughing and joking with colleagues the entire time. Jonas couldn't believe how much of a different person he was. Rina hadn't wanted to attend, but her husband dragged her. He said she would regret it if she didn't come. After what had happened with Jenny a few months prior, she had lost interest in pubs, and many social functions. Besides her patients, Rina found talking to people uninteresting as well.

Rina would come to regret that night, but for the opposite reason to what her husband thought. She wished she'd never gone. She had respected Adam Greber for the psychiatrist he was, a legend in his own right. She respected him still even after he awarded Sarah Alloy the position.

She lost respect for him after the words he shared with her on that night, though. Jonas was laughing with some colleagues on the other side of the bar. His close friend Caleb Janson was the loudest in the group, as usual. Rina found Caleb to be an exhausting person to be around. Jonas loved the man. Caleb was a surgeon at Holy Saints. For a man who saved many lives, Rina found him insufferable. Everything about him was... loud.

For that reason, she sat at a table by herself, a pint of beer in front of her. She didn't really drink it. It was mostly a prop to fit in. She had made Jonas promise to leave the party after an hour and a half of being there. It was already close to their agreed-upon time, but you wouldn't have known from how much fun Jonas appeared to be having.

"Want a drink, Rina?" She looked up and saw Cody Alder from the psych ward smiling at her.

"I'm fine, Cody, thanks," she replied.

Cody nodded and went back to the bar where Adam Greber was having a shot with Cody's father, Ron, a member of management at Holy Saints. Rina didn't know Ron that well, besides the nasty comments Jonas made about him. Rina was surprised at his remarks given that Ron Alder had been invited to their wedding. Jonas said he invited all of management to the wedding to make more connections.

Dr. Greber spotted Rina glancing their way. He stumbled to her and sat, making an incredibly loud noise with the chair when he pulled it out.

"What do you want first, Rina?" Adam Greber asked. "My words to you on my last day as your boss, or my words as your friend?"

Rina was taken back by his question but answered it. "My friend."

Adam fixed his glasses. "You are one of the finest psychiatrist I have ever met. In the short time we worked together, I've seen you do incredible work, but after what happened with Jenny, you're not the same. You stopped trying. You're... depressed. You're... not present anymore."

Rina laughed uncomfortably at him, taking a long drink of her beer. "And what do you have to say as my boss?"

Adam gulped his beer, wiping his mouth with his sleeve. "Get help or get a new job."

Rina lay on her couch thinking about what she would have said to Adam Greber that night if she could have gone back in time. Many times, it was cuss words. Sometimes it was a professional answer. Sometimes she took his offer.

Rina wished she could go back in time and take back

what she actually said. After she finished making a scene, Adam Greber stood up from her table and continued to drink with his willing and able colleagues, including Jonas.

Despite that night being his retirement party, he would work another few months as part of a last-minute extension. Sarah was to take his place, but hospital management thought more time was needed for the transition. Adam agreed to the terms, unfortunately. The next few months she tried to avoid talking to Adam Greber as much as she could. He seemed to pick up on her frustration but didn't care less. He was on his way out. Rina would be Sarah's problem now, not his.

Rina could feel tension in her hand and realized she was clenching her fist in anger. Even after finding out he was murdered, she was still angry with him for what he'd said.

She tried to shut her eyes, and sleep. She had another midnight shift on the ward and would need rest. She was accustomed to only having a few hours of broken sleep, and after the news about Adam, she knew it would be even less today.

Eventually she moved from the couch to the bed, Denzel slowly getting up and moving with her. She rolled in her sheets, restlessly. She opened her eyes at one point to find that she had been attempting to sleep for nearly an hour with no success. She stood up and fixed her black-out curtains. She plopped back into bed and shut her eyes, trying her best to clear her mind. For a moment she thought she'd found some peace and was drifting asleep.

Rina opened her eyes suddenly and stood up. She looked outside her curtains at the bright light shining in. Working overnights was tough even on the best of days. She knew she needed more to clear her mind.

She grabbed her runners and changed into light clothes. Denzel waged his tail, but Rina didn't feel up to bringing him on the run. She felt overwhelmed with emotions she didn't completely understand herself. She opened her front door and ran down the block. She smiled when she felt her lungs begin to tire after running for over ten minutes.

She ran past the small downtown center of Carrington. The four blocks of the center of town included a municipal building, a few strip malls of local shop owners and an old motel. Rina was surprised the motel managed to stay in business since she never saw any vehicles in its parking lot. If the inside of the rooms looked as run-down as the outside, she wouldn't think it would have much repeat business either.

A few cars passed the intersection as Rina waited for her turn to cross. A blue car turned down the street and she immediately noticed Sarah Alloy driving.

Rina quickly turned her head in the opposite direction, hoping Sarah hadn't seen her. She looked and the blue car had passed her and didn't appear to slow. The signal finally went on for Rina to walk and she ran across the street.

After some time, the light began to lessen. The cloudy sky turned greyer. Rina thought about turning around, but knew she had a goal when she went out her door. She wouldn't go home until she completed it.

She turned down another street and was soon at Adam Greber's front door. The door was bright red, with yellow police tape across it.

Rina knocked loudly, but nobody answered. She knocked again, and the front door creaked open. She wondered what she would say to Adam's wife if she was home.

Rina called out into the empty house but heard nothing. She carefully extended her leg between the yellow tape and entered the building. She called again, this time yelling for Adam by name, but heard nothing.

Shuffling in the living room caught her attention. She called out for Adam as she entered. The floor felt slippery under her shoes. She looked at the bottom of her foot and her white shoe was covered in red. She looked at the floor again and found she had stepped in a puddle of blood.

Rina heard the shuffling sound again coming from behind the couch.

"Adam!" she yelled. The shuffling sound stopped, and the

room was silent. "Adam, come out."

A small hand reached from behind the couch and waved. The shuffling sound started again, until she saw the lumpy mass of a set of arms and feet slide across the floor, leaving a trail of blood behind it. Then it popped its head from around the couch, smiling.

"Jenny!" Rina shouted.

Rina woke up in her bed, her heart racing, gasping for breath. She wiped the sweat from her forehead and calmed herself. She got out of bed quickly, taking a moment to look into her living room. Denzel stood up on her mattress and walked in a circle before lying down again.

This wasn't her first nightmare that had had Jenny in it. It wouldn't be her last. She cursed herself for not doing something about it. How long would the young girl haunt her nights?

Rina knew she couldn't stay in her house any longer. She decided to go to work early, even if it was by several hours.

When she entered the ward, she headed straight to her office. If she was lucky, she could get there before anyone noticed she was there and lock the door behind her. As she hustled down the hall, she noticed Nurse Bethany talking loudly to a patient. She also saw her – Amy, sitting at the same desk, her journal clenched between her thighs, working on a puzzle. Even though Rina wasn't close enough to hear, she knew Amy was humming that tune. The playground rhyme she always sang to herself.

Rina turned her head and continued at a quick pace down the hall. She opened her door as the office across the hall opened, and Sarah came out with a Kleenex in her hand.

She wiped her eyes when she spotted Rina.

"I tried to call you," Sarah said.

"Jonas told me what happened," Rina said, knowing what Sarah meant. "How are you doing?"

Sarah smiled, a new tear forming in her eye. "A mess, to be honest. It's been a hard day on the ward. I was about to leave to go home. Belinda said she was fine taking your overnight shift tonight too. It's a lot for her to do, but she wants to make sure we're supported during this time."

Rina nodded. "That's nice of Belinda, but I'm coming in early to work. I can't stay at home. I feel better here."

"That makes sense for you," she said with a smile. Her grin quickly vanished. "I still can't believe someone did that to him." She looked around the empty hall. "Murdered him in his kitchen like that," she whispered.

Rina raised an eyebrow. "It happened in his kitchen? How did you know that? I tried to look online but couldn't find anything."

Sarah wiped her tears. "I... don't want to talk about it anymore. I can't handle this. I'm going to go home for the night. I'll try my best to be better tomorrow, and not a snotty mess."

Rina nodded again. "It's understandable, Sarah."

"He was... a good man," she said. "He had his flaws, like all of us, but for the most part he was a good mentor... to both of us."

"He was," Rina agreed.

Sarah took a few steps down the hall but looked back at her. "There was a detective wanting to talk to you, by the way. I told him you didn't work till night. He might come back, he said."

"Okay, thanks."

Sarah shook her head and wiped her eyes again. "That detective. Hicks, I think he said his name was. I've never thought poorly of a police officer before, but he was nasty."

CHAPTER 9

Rina sat in her office for over an hour before a knock startled her out of a half-awake state.

"Come in," she said. For a moment there was silence and so she repeated it at a yell.

Belinda shyly opened the door and walked inside. "Hey," she said awkwardly, sitting in the chair in front of the desk. "I talked to Sarah today. If you need time to yourself, Rina, it's completely understandable. I can hold the fort tonight for everyone."

"I do better at work."

"Okay, but it's okay if you change your mind. I'm not done with work for another two hours, so you have more time to think about it. It wouldn't upset me if you did."

"I won't," Rina said with a smile. "Everyone doing well today on the ward?"

Belinda nodded. "Nothing too much to report on." She went over a few patients of Rina's. Just as her colleague had said, there wasn't anything too concerning happening.

"How about... Jenny? Anything new with her? How is she doing at the ward so far?"

"You mean Amy?" Belinda corrected. "We don't have a Jenny here."

"Sorry," Rina said. "I must be losing my mind tonight. Yes, Amy Deaver. How is she?"

"I'm getting nowhere with her, to be honest. I mean, what can I do, she won't speak. Do you have any recommendations?"

"I'm sure you're doing everything you can, Belinda. I'm not sure how I could add much more."

Belinda sat up in her chair. "Well, I know you were really good at connecting to some of the more... difficult patients we've had here. I would love your opinion on her case. If you want some reading material tonight, I left her file on my desk in my office; help yourself."

"Okay, but I'm not sure what I could give you pointers on."

"I just got off the phone with Phyllis Deaver, giving her an update too." Belinda sighed. "Like I said, not much we can do for her. If she continues to be calm like how she is on the ward, then we can give Phyllis a safety plan for her niece and look to discharge soon."

"How did Phyllis take the news?" Rina asked, knowing the answer.

"I've never spoken to someone so condescending," Belinda said with a harsh tone. "If she wasn't so big in this hospital for some reason, I'd tell her off. She even went as far as to say if her niece ends up back at the ward, or worse, in the morgue, she will blame me personally. I mean, she's a doctor, a pediatrician! How can she talk to us that way?"

"She's always been a piece of work," Rina agreed. "There was a nurse, a young woman, I forget her name. Anyway, she worked with Dr. Deaver at the pedia clinic for about a month. In that short time she filed for a stress leave due to the harassment she received from Phyllis. She never returned to work as a nurse. I heard she quit the occupation altogether and is working as a teacher now. It's a rumor, though, that Jonas told me." Rina twinged when she caught herself saying his name. "Anyway, nothing we say can appease Phyllis Deaver, so why bother?"

Belinda nodded. "The worst part is, I worry Deaver's right to be upset with us. The girl could go home and hurt herself again. We can tell Phyllis to keep her medications locked away as well as the knives and anything else she could harm herself with, but Amy could find a way. She's not dumb. Look at the work she's done with those puzzles. She's already finished all of them and is doing them over again from scratch. She just sits there all day, hums that song, and works on a puzzle. I know her mother homeschooled her. I would love to find out more about Amy's intellectual capabilities."

"What about medications for her?"

Belinda shook her head. "Phyllis is against them. Amy won't give us permission, since she's not verbal, and won't even sign a form. She's eighteen but Phyllis is her guardian with her mother... gone. It's so terrible – her mother vanished and living on your own with a woman like Phyllis Deaver. Who can blame her for being in here." She laughed to herself.

"Well, you've basically given me all the details, and I'm with you. What else can you do?"

"Thanks for listening. I still worry about Amy, though. She's so young. I'd hate to hear something had happened to her after she's been discharged. I would really struggle if I found out—" She stopped talking suddenly and looked at Rina, embarrassed. "Never mind. Well, I'm going to finish a few reports. If you need something from me, I'll be in my office."

Rina nodded, and before Belinda could leave, she called out to her. "By the way, Belinda, I think you're doing a good job here."

Belinda smiled. "Thanks. That means a lot. Have a good night, and like I said, if you change your mind about working tonight, come find me."

Rina thanked her again and her colleague left, leaving her alone in her office once more. Rina rose and turned off the light, locking the door. She sat at her desk again, in the dark, taking in deep breaths.

"Get help," Adam Greber had told her, "or get a new job."

Rina laid her head on the desk, and tried to rest again. She wasn't sure why she'd come to work early. She wished she had gotten past her nightmare and stayed at home with Denzel. She remained in her office until she knew Belinda would have left for the night.

She opened her office door and snuck out. The patients

were already in their rooms for the night, and she saw Nurse Bethany and Cody walking down the hall. With everyone shut away except for staff, every footstep in the hall echoed.

"There you are," Cody said. "We checked the workout room, looking for you."

"I stopped by ER to consult on a case," Rina lied. "Everything okay?"

"Everyone is accounted for," Nurse Bethany said. "Everyone is in their rooms, and meds have been given with no issues."

"Thanks for the update. I'll do my own room check though."

The nurses exchanged a glance. Cody nodded. "No problem. I got a fifteen-minute break, though. I'll be outside."

"Enjoy your time," Rina said with a smile, passing them.

It was typical that only patients who were suicidal would have scheduled room checks at night, but Rina felt the need to look in on everyone. She took her time checking each patient in their room to ensure they were sleeping. Most were. The ones who weren't were used to someone opening their slot and wouldn't pay attention to staff. Rina would greet them if they were awake before shutting the slot.

Finally, she got to Amy's room. Rina took a deep breath before opening her slot. Just as the night before, the girl was passed out. The notebook she carried everywhere was clamped between her forearms as she slept on her side.

She shut the slot slowly, attempting not to make a noise, but failed; it made a loud metal screech. As the slot slid closed, the girl sat up in her bed, holding the journal to her chest, staring at Rina.

Rina didn't greet Amy before closing her slot completely. She turned and walked back down the hall towards her office. She could finish the room checks later, she told herself.

"Hey," she heard from down a dim hallway. She saw Cody coming towards her. He used his fingers to brush back his medium length curly black hair. Even though he was down the hall, she could already smell his strong cologne, which was against the ward's rules to wear.

"Cody," Rina said. "What's up?"

"How are you doing? You know, with Adam?" he asked, staring at her intently. Rina hated how he looked at her. It was almost as if he assumed she would break down and cry and fling herself at him.

"It's terrible what happened," Rina said. "How about you?"

"My father knew him well. I would see him around our home sometimes, but I didn't speak to him much." He reached out and grabbed Rina's hand. "We work in mental health but that doesn't mean we don't need help too sometimes. You can tell me anything you want, and I'll listen." He looked down the empty hallway. "We could go to your office if you want. Nobody will bother us there. We can chat."

Rina pulled her arm away, feeling some resistance from him when she did. "I think I've had enough of this. I don't think I've ever given you a reason to think I'm into you, but I can see your intentions clear as day. Please stop."

"Rina, we don't have to—"

"Dr. Kent, please," she reminded him. "Please speak to me only in professional terms. We work on the ward together. I know we run a skeleton crew at night, but I would still appreciate you speaking to me in professional terms."

He scoffed. "They were right about you."

Rina could feel her blood pressure rising. "That's enough. I don't care what people say about me, or what you think of me. Don't touch me again in the way you did tonight. If you do, I will file a complaint so quickly with HR that even your daddy won't be able to save you. Now, please finish room checks. I got up to Amy's room."

Cody scoffed again and went down the hall, shaking his head to himself. "I wasn't coming on to you, *Dr. Kent*," he said as he walked away. "You need help."

At that moment she wished she had the power to

terminate him on the spot. She collected herself and continued towards her office.

What a pig, she thought. Rina had a sense of what the young nurse wanted from her, and it had nothing to do with consoling her. The last thing he wanted was to save Rina. He was only thinking of himself. She wondered how much his dad, who was also a part of management at the hospital, influenced Adam Greber when he was hiring a new psychiatric nurse on the ward.

She stopped when she passed Belinda's office. She took a deep breath as she twisted the doorknob. Just as Dr. Knowles said, she'd left it open. On the desk was a stack of paperwork, topped with a folder titled "Deaver, Amy".

She was about to grab the file when she noticed a picture frame of Belinda on the desk. Beside Belinda in the picture was Adam Greber, his arm wrapped around her. Both had large smiles. It was weird seeing the age contrast between the two, Belinda being over thirty years younger than him.

Rina hadn't even known they knew each other. Adam did assist Sarah in hiring Belinda, but other than that, Rina assumed she and Adam Greber weren't close colleagues. You certainly wouldn't get that impression looking at the photo on her desk, though.

A Kleenex box was beside the frame, and several scrunched up used ones were in a waste basket below.

Rina grabbed Amy's file and left the office, looking one last time at the picture of Adam and Belinda before closing the door.

CHAPTER 10

Rina sat at her desk, flopping the file folder in front of her. The sound of rain hitting the windowpane distracted her a moment. She looked outside at the rolling lightning shooting across the sky like a fireworks display. She wondered when the storms would stop. It felt like it had been raining non-stop for the past several days now.

She looked back at the file and took a deep breath. She opened the beige cover and took out the batch of stapled documents.

Holy Saints Intake Form. Rina read the details, including Amy's date of birth and current address, which was her aunt's home. The sloppy handwriting showed that Sarah had filled out the form. Typically, intake forms would include a lot based on what the patient shared. This report had very little. Rina read it in a few minutes.

Patient dressed in grey sweatpants and white shirt. Hair disheveled. Patient was recently discharged from E.R. by Dr. Jonas Kent, the attending physician, who reported that her toxicology reports are now normal. Her system was flushed following an overdose of acetaminophen and ibuprofen.

Patient is mute through the interview. She has not expressed much emotion and has only made eye contact with interviewers for short durations. At times she does sing a wordless song of some kind, but the interviewer is not aware of the tune's origin. Patient's aunt, Dr. Phyllis Deaver, reports that the patient has autism, and has been mute for some time.

Review attached interview with temporary guardian, Phyllis Deaver. Patient has brought with her a blue journal, which was found on her person by paramedics. Patient doesn't wish to let staff see what she has written in her book and appears guarded when asked. Patient appears to have a calm demeanor. Not responding to questions on suicide.

The intake note was much shorter than usual, but Amy Deaver hadn't given them much to go off of besides presentation and what brought her to Holy Saints. Rina thought it was interesting that Jonas didn't mention providing care to Amy when he saw him last.

Rina turned to the attached interview with Phyllis Deaver, a form also filled by Sarah.

Intake Interview with Patient's Aunt and temporary guardian, Phyllis Deaver. For the sake of transparency, the writer will mention that Dr. Phyllis Deaver is a pediatrician at Holy Saints Hospital. Professional titles will not be included in the remainder of the report.

Mrs. Deaver reports that her niece has been living with her for the past several years. Mrs. Deaver reports no incidents of suicide attempts or ideation in the past. Mrs. Deaver reports that the patient's mother, Marie, has been missing for over a month. Unfortunately, police have closed the missing persons case, Mrs. Deaver reports.

Mrs. Deaver reports that the patient was not always mute, but known to verbally communicate mostly with her mother. After the disappearance of Marie Deaver, the patient has remained mute entirely, Mrs. Deaver reports.

While the patient has been mute, Mrs. Deaver reports that she is keenly aware of her surroundings, and is functionally able to care for herself hygienically, and complete chores such as cleaning, and preparing non-cooked meals for herself.

Patient will at times write messages on paper, however Mrs. Deaver reports that she has not communicated to her in some time in this way. Mrs. Deaver reports that Patient has a journal that she writes in occasionally. Patient doesn't allow others to see what she writes, including Mrs. Deaver.

Mrs. Deaver has advised that she is available at any time for updates or questions from clinical staff.

Rina leaned back in her chair. She could feel Phyllis Deaver's concerns over her niece even through the written words of Dr. Alloy. Rina shook her head. When Phyllis cornered her on the staircase, she knew she was concerned for her niece then too. Rina had almost blown her off in frustration.

"Get help or get a new job," Adam Greber had told Rina. She took a deep breath. She hated herself at times for feeling as empty as she did. All she wanted to do was work and spend time with Denzel at home. At work, all Rina wanted to do was coast. Get through her day. Make sure at the end of the day nobody had... hurt themself.

How much had Rina distanced herself from the good work she used to do at Holy Saints? The *old* Dr. Rina Kent would have already had some ideas of how to connect with a girl like Amy. Even now, reading Amy's file, she had been tempted several times to put everything back on Belinda's desk and pretend she never looked at it. Why get involved? She wouldn't be able to help. She couldn't even help herself.

She looked at the last page of the stapled report. It was a clinical chart note from Belinda.

Writer sat with patient in a quiet room to allow for no distractions. Writer allowed patient to work on a puzzle during clinical time. Writer hoped this would have helped with patient feeling more comfortable in speaking or communicating in some way. Writer wrote a message to patient on a piece of paper and put it in front of her to read. Patient did not respond to written communication and continued with completing her puzzle. Writer ended the session after fifteen minutes due to lack of engagement. Patient was hygienically clean for the session and dressed appropriately. Her demeanor was calm throughout.

There were two other entries from Belinda, but each had similar outcomes. Amy Deaver didn't say a word.

Rina would have pulled her hair out in frustration if she had Amy as a patient. She almost wanted to close the file and go back to staring out the window and relax to the sound of rain against the pane.

She remembered what Belinda told her before leaving. They planned to release Amy Deaver soon with a safety plan and the hope nothing worse would happen.

Rina looked outside her window. She had always admired her view of the thick forest that surrounded the hospital. The trees swayed in the heavy wind of the storm. A bolt of lightning struck down in the distance. She turned to the side to get a view of the employee parking lot.

She thought of Jenny Berange. What would Rina have done differently that day had she known what the girl planned to do? Rina knew she would have tried harder. She would have listened better. She would have given that girl her full attention.

Amy Deaver needed Rina's attention now.

What did Amy like to do at home? What were her interests? What did she write about?

Amy was homeschooled by her mother, Marie Deaver. There could be so much to learn from her mother, but the only person who knew Amy well was missing. All that gave Rina was Phyllis Deaver.

Rina could talk to her. Perhaps she could arrange for a group interview with Phyllis, herself and Belinda.

The thought of getting involved in Amy's case ignited something inside Rina. She almost felt how she had when she started working at her first psych ward practicum in Calgary as a student. She smiled.

If Phyllis didn't have much information, they could ask her to go into Amy's bedroom and get some ideas. Rina took out a notepad and wrote down some of her thoughts. She wrote the word "dad" and underlined it.

Who was Amy's father? Would he be able to give any more information?

Rina raised her head and smiled again. Phyllis Deaver had

lived in Carrington since she was a child. Rina assumed the same for her sister. There was a good chance that Amy was even born at Holy Saints.

Rina turned on her laptop and opened the patient health records system. She searched for Marie Deaver. A few documents loaded on the screen. Some were in relation to a rotator cuff tear surgery she had with Dr. Janson. The reports suggested that Marie had been hiking ten years ago when she slipped and fell, injuring her shoulder.

Next was a record of Amy Deaver's birth. Rina frowned. No mention of a father had been inputted in the system. A nurse's note only mentioned Phyllis Deaver visiting and assisting with care. Rina smiled when she read that Phyllis had demanded the nurse write in her note that she officially complained that her sister was not provided sufficient visits to Marie's room. As a result, the nurse had documented how long she visited each time she saw Marie and newly born Amy Deaver. Even when her sister was giving birth, Phyllis was not able to control herself.

Rina closed that note. The last entry from hospital records almost made her mouth drop. It was a file from Adam Greber.

Marie Deaver was a patient? Sarah and Belinda haven't mentioned it. The record was dated almost nine years ago. It was well before Sarah, Belinda or Rina started working at Holy Saints.

She attempted to open the record but a message popped up: the file was password-protected. At times, patients' records were kept confidential from other staff if the patients worked at the hospital or were related to someone who worked there. It wasn't uncommon not to be able to open relatives' health records without permission. What was weird, though, was that Rina could access everything except Adam Greber's reporting.

Rina would bring this up with Belinda and Sarah in the morning when they arrived. They needed to get the reporting from when Amy's mother was on the ward. Even though Amy would have only been nine or ten years old when her mother was admitted, it could give more insight on Amy herself.

A loud knock on Rina's office door startled her, and she dropped the file folder on the ground. Her office door opened, and an older man in a dark suit entered her office. He said nothing for a moment, furrowing his thick eyebrows at Rina.

"Are you Dr. Kent?" the man asked.

Rina caught her breath at the man's sudden appearance. "Yes, who are you?"

The man dug into his white dress shirt and removed a gold shield that hung around his neck. "Detective Cormac Hicks. I had asked your boss to tell you I would be wanting to speak to you."

Rina looked at her laptop's screen. "It's nearly five in the morning."

"And time's ticking, Mrs. Kent," he said with a grunt. "Sorry, Dr. Kent. When someone is murdered it's important to get all the information you can from anyone who had connections."

Rina was taken back by how crass Detective Hicks was. She expected a cop to talk differently. Rina had the distinct impression he wasn't the type to waste time with pleasantries.

"How can I help you, detective?" she asked.

The detective nodded. "How well did you know Adam Greber?"

"Just in a work capacity... I suppose," Rina answered. "He was Chief of Psychiatry at the hospital for a long time. I worked for him until he retired."

"Was he a... good man, would you say?"

"I guess so."

"When was the last time you talked to or saw Adam Greber?" Detective Hicks made a clicking sound from the side of his mouth. He leaned forward in the chair towards Rina.

She tried to calm her nerves. Her breath was fast. The cop had an intimidating presence. She tried her best to think of an answer.

"His last day at work was only a few weeks ago. I think it was that day."

"You think?" Detective Hicks said with a harsh tone. "Or do you know that to be fact?"

"It's a small town. Sometimes you run into people shopping, or whatever. I don't think I had any meaningful conversations with Adam if I did see him."

Detective Hicks leaned back in his chair, removing a small notepad from his suit pocket. He flipped through a few pages, squinting to read. "Adam Greber had a retirement party. Did you attend?"

Rina nodded. "We all did."

"At that party it seems you and him had some type of altercation."

"I wouldn't call it that," Rina said.

"And what would you call it, then?" Hicks said, making the clicking sound with his mouth again.

Rina shifted and took in a deep breath. "I was upset with what he said. He wasn't happy with my... work performance. I didn't like how he expressed himself."

"That's what I hear as well," the detective said. He flipped another page. "It was reported that he told you that you needed professional help. Why would he say that?"

She slumped in her chair. She had thought nobody had heard him say that to her. Rina thought of the picture of Adam with his arm draped around Belinda.

"I was struggling with the death of a patient," Rina admitted.

"Right," Detective Hicks said, "I heard that. And what was your response to Adam Greber when he said that to you at the party?"

Rina lowered her head, knowing the answer. "I don't... remember."

"Go to hell," Detective Hicks said with a harsh tone. He smiled. "Hey, sometimes I hate my boss too. How much did you hate Adam Greber?"

"I didn't hate him," Rina said, raising her voice.

"Right, you just wanted him to go to hell," Detective Hicks said slyly. "What about after he demoted you?"

Rina shook her head, biting her lip. "He didn't demote me. I applied for his job, but I didn't get it."

Detective Hicks flipped a few more pages in his notebook. "And now Sarah Alloy is your boss?"

Rina raised her head and looked at the cop sternly, annoyed by his games. "Sarah is a good psychiatrist. She deserved the position she was rewarded."

"So, you don't want Sarah to go to hell too?" Detective Hicks asked. He smiled and didn't give her a chance to answer. "After telling Adam Greber to go to hell at his retirement party, do you remember what you said immediately after to your new boss?"

Rina lowered her head. She knew. She could almost remember their drunken faces when she barked it at them "I told Sarah, Jenny Berange's suicide was her fault." Rina looked up at the detective. "The table shouldn't have been in the rec area."

Detective Hicks nodded. "That's what I have too. You must get along well now that Sarah is your new boss. Can you tell me what you've done for the past two days? Give me a breakdown of everywhere you went. Anything you did."

"I was at the hospital, working. When I wasn't working, I was at home. That's it."

"Right, and you never left the property at all? For a coffee or drive through, anything?"

"I didn't. Are we almost done here?" Rina said with a harsh tone. The detective no longer scared her. She was becoming more offended by his presence now.

"Almost," the detective said. "You never texted Adam Greber, or called him after he retired?"

"That's right, I didn't. Like I just said, I haven't seen or communicated with him in some time."

"Then you wouldn't mind showing me your phone and opening your last conversation with Adam Greber then?"

Rina leaned back in her chair now. "I don't legally have to."

"You don't. If you care about me finding the killer of your ex-boss, you will, though. Then I can move on and bother someone else. Leave you alone."

Rina breathed out and grabbed her phone. She opened Adam's contact and showed the detective.

"No calls and no messages," Hicks said. "You never talked to your boss after work?"

"We only talked at work," Rina said.

Detective Hicks stood up from the chair, patting away a piece of white fluff that had attached itself to his jacket. "And retirement parties apparently. So—" He looked at Rina sternly. "—did you listen to your boss? Did you get help for yourself?"

Rina felt rage building inside her. "I was able to use my skills to alleviate my symptoms myself."

The detective smiled. "Would have been something to see. A psychiatrist who needs their own psychiatrist."

Rina perked up in her chair at the comment. "Nobody is bulletproof, detective. Everyone's mental health can be vulnerable."

Detective Hicks smacked the middle of his chest, which made a dull sound. "Well, in my case I am bulletproof. Unfortunately, someone knew Adam Greber wasn't… Dr. Kent, please don't leave Carrington for the next little while if you could. That's not a demand, but it could be helpful for my investigation. I may need to speak with you again."

CHAPTER 11

After the detective left her office, Rina waited, fuming in her chair. Was that what they called "bad cop"? she wondered.

She thought police officers held themselves in a more professional way. Detective Cormac Hicks had been anything but. She hoped he hadn't pressed Adam Gerber's wife in the same fashion.

Vanessa Greber was not a woman known for keeping her emotions tight. At a Christmas party she remembered Vanessa crying as they sang Christmas carols. A man like Detective Hicks would traumatize her.

She stood up and grabbed her gym bag. She required a run to cool down. Her phone vibrated on her desk. Rina picked it up and saw a message from Jonas and opened it.

"Can we meet up?" he texted. "I'm at the hospital right now on a midnight. I heard you are too. Maybe we can meet up in the cafeteria when you have a break. It's slow tonight for a change. Let me know."

Rina shook her head. The last thing she wanted to torture herself with was another conversation with Jonas. She tossed her phone in her bag and headed for the gym outside the ward.

When she swiped her pass, a green light appeared, and she opened the doors. Ryan, the security guard, nearly jumped in his seat in his guard station. She wondered how long he had been *alert* for.

"Hey, Dr. Kent," he said to her. Rina nodded back. The lights in the hall flickered a moment. "Some storm we're having." He smiled. "Have a good workout."

"Thanks," Rina said, annoyed at him attempting to pretend she didn't notice how poorly he was doing at his job.

Rina took her time in the changing room, thinking about everything that had just happened.

Marie Deaver was a psych patient under Adam Greber.

Adam Greber was murdered in his home the same day Amy Deaver was admitted to the ward.

It could mean nothing, Rina knew. Likely it was nothing. She changed into her workout gear and headed straight for the treadmill. She placed her duffle bag beside the machine and stepped on, clicking it to start. She warmed up for several minutes before beginning to sprint.

The lights in the room flickered again. Rina ignored everything around her. She gazed at the cement wall in front as ran.

If only she could find a way to access Adam Greber's reporting from when Marie was a patient. Then Rina could be sure there was no connection at all.

Suddenly the lights turned off. The machine lost power immediately and she straightened her legs, feeling pain from the jolt of stopping while sprinting.

The room was pitch dark. The new hospital couldn't come soon enough, she thought. Why would anybody choose to be admitted to Holy Saints with conditions like this? She knew why. It was surrounded by a large rural community, and they lacked options.

She bent down in the darkness to grab her phone from her duffle bag, patting around the machine until she touched it.

The gym door screeched open. The red lights in the hall lightened the room for a moment, and the door slammed shut.

"Ryan?" Rina called out into the darkness. Nothing answered, except a footstep. A moment after, she heard the clink on the floor of another step towards her.

Rina quickly opened her duffle bag and clicked the side of her phone. The blue screen dimly lit the room. Rina waved it around until she saw Amy Deaver.

She slowly took several more steps towards Rina. Rina held her breath. The blue light against the girl made her pale skin look grey. Her arms were criss-crossed around her chest, with her journal tight between her fingers.

The girl took another step towards her. Rina managed to finally find the words.

"Amy!" she called out to her. "What are you doing? How did you get out of the ward?"

"Adam Greber," the girl whispered. Her eyes were wide as she stared at Rina.

"What?"

The girl took another step towards her. "Adam Greber," she whispered again. "Ronald Alder, Phyllis Deaver." Amy tightened her grip around her journal. "Jonas Kent."

Rina stood up. The lights beamed bright in the room again, the power being fully restored. It blinded her for a moment. Amy covered her eyes with her forearm.

"Why did you say those names?" Rina asked. "Why? How do you know Jonas? Why did you say 'Adam Greber'?"

Amy removed her arm and stared at Rina again. "Adam Greber, Ronald Alder, Phyllis Deaver, Jonas Kent." The door to the gym opened and Ryan ran into the room. "Say nothing," Amy whispered.

CHAPTER 12

Rina stared at the incident report she had to file regarding Amy leaving the ward. It had been several hours, and she hadn't written a word, not sure what to say. Sarah and Belinda walked into her office. Belinda had a smile on her face and put her expensive latte on Rina's desk. Sarah had a more serious look, her eyebrows furrowed.

"Well," Belinda said. "Sounds like you had an interesting night shift."

Rina feigned a smile back. "Who told you?"

"The security guard," Sarah answered. "How did she get out?"

Rina shook her head. "During the storm there was another outage. She must have gotten out of her room and through the ward doors, slipping past the ever so alert security guard."

Belinda nodded. "Why would she run off the ward into the gym though?"

Rina shrugged.

Sarah sat at the other side of the desk and leaned forward. "What did she say to you?"

Rina looked down at her report and pretended not to hear what her boss had asked. Why did Amy say those names to her? Why was one of them her ex-husband's? What did it mean?

"Nothing," she lied. "She didn't say a word."

Belinda nodded, but Sarah didn't seem happy with the answer. "That's not what Ryan said. He said he heard the girl whisper something to you when he went into the gym."

Rina shook her head. "I wish she had spoken." She looked at Belinda. "I read her notes last night like you asked. That would have been a huge breakthrough. Ryan, as I said before, was barely alert. I think I caught him sleeping last night when I went to the gym. I don't think he was hearing right, or fully awake for that matter."

"It's not the first issue we have had with that guard, as you know. I'll talk to his superior." Sarah pursed her lips. "It doesn't make sense. Why would she go to the gym? She just... wanted to see what the room was? She didn't do anything once she was inside?"

Belinda smiled. "Would have been something if she started doing push-ups." Sarah ignored the joke. Belinda took a sip of coffee and looked at Rina. "So, she walked into the gym, saw you, and then what? What happened?"

Rina lowered her head. She looked at the empty report as if it could give her answers. "She hummed that tune. That nursery rhyme or whatever that song is."

Belinda shook in her seat. "I know I shouldn't feel this way, but it honestly creeps me out how she does that all day."

"Thanks for clearing that up, Rina," Sarah said. "Anything else to report?"

Rina shook her head.

"Well, go ahead and head home after you fill out the incident report for her file. I think we can count this as our patient roundup for the day. Were you okay after what happened?"

Rina stared at her boss, trying to find the words. "Fine. I'm fine. She just... startled me when the lights were off,"

Belinda took another sip of her coffee. "I can't wait for the new hospital. They need to demolish this building right after we move out. Nothing works, not even the electrical."

They left Rina's office and Sarah asked Rina to drop in the handwritten incident report before she left. Sarah promised again to speak to security's management about the concern over

Ryan.

Once they'd left, Rina lowered her head. Why didn't she say what Amy said to her? What had Jonas done that made him a part of the list with the other names? What connection did Jonas have with Amy Deaver?

Rina sat in silence, trying to think of a connection. She tried to think even harder on why she was lying about what happened. All the names on the list worked at Holy Saints. Could that be the only connection between them?

Rina struck her desk with her fist in anger. She could have said what Amy had whispered to her in the gym. It would have made more sense. Rina began writing the report. She tried to remember everything she had told Belinda and Sarah to maintain the lies.

What was her ex-husband not telling her? She needed to know. She had already lied about what happened. She may as well hear Jonas's side first.

Belinda knocked on Rina's office door again. "Sorry, I forgot my coffee." She stepped in and grabbed her cup off the desk. "Thanks for looking at Amy's file for me. Did you have any notes that you took, anything you think I could do? I almost wish Amy said something to you last night."

Rina feigned another smile. "Me too. No notes for you. I think you have done everything I would have tried."

"Well, have a good morning. See you tonight."

"Wait, did Sarah mention to you much about Amy's mother?"

Belinda shook her head. "Not really. Just that she has been missing for over a month. Apparently, and this is just rumors, the mom moved to a large city. It's sad. She left her only daughter to Phyllis."

"Seems like Phyllis cares about her," Rina injected.

Belinda nodded. "At least we got one impossible answer from Amy. Does Phyllis Deaver have emotions like a regular human being? Apparently so... Why do you ask about Marie Deaver?"

"Well… I looked on the online portal for medical records. Apparently, Amy's mother was a patient on our ward about nine years ago. Her primary psychiatrist was Adam Greber."

Belinda raised an eyebrow. "Really? I wonder if Sarah knows that. You should have mentioned that earlier."

Rina shrugged. "It escaped me. What happened with Amy last night really threw me off."

"I wonder."

"What?"

Belinda looked at Rina, surprised. "Is this something we should tell that cop, Detective Hicks?" Belinda shook her head. "I mean… never mind. I'm not sure why I said that."

Rina thought about the framed picture in Belinda Knowles' office of Adam and her. "You two were close, weren't you?"

Belinda looked down at a stain on the desk. "I made a mess with my coffee. Do you have any wipes?"

Rina opened a drawer and grabbed a tissue for the table, giving it to Belinda.

"I didn't know that you knew him well," she said.

"He… was a good mentor," Belinda said. "I just want… whoever did this needs to be found."

"He was your mentor? How did you know Adam? I assumed you didn't have a connection before the ward."

Belinda smiled. "He teaches part-time at the U of C in Calgary, as I'm sure you know. He was instrumental in my education. He hired me too. I was one of his best students." Belinda lowered her head. "I can't tell you the amount of time I spent in his office at the university, trying to do better in his class. He not only helped me in his class, but my degree in general. I could always count on his support. I heard… that after taking a small break when he retired from the ward, he was going to keep teaching part-time at the university. Maybe even take a larger role at the faculty there. The kids coming up don't know what they'll be missing… Sorry." Belinda wiped her tears with the Kleenex. "I'll need another tissue for your desk now," she said with a chuckle. "Well, you're tired and probably want to get going. I'll leave you with your report and see you tonight."

"By the way, did you have the pleasure of talking to Detective Hicks yet?" Rina asked, shaking her head.

Belinda nodded. "He spoke with a lot of staff yesterday."

"He actually came back to the ward early this morning. He grilled me on Adam Greber. I never expected a detective to talk the way he did."

Belinda laughed. "Really? I thought Detective Hicks was really pleasant, actually."

CHAPTER 13

Rina made her way quickly down the hall, her completed incident report in her hand. She planned on dropping it off on Sarah's desk before leaving. Rina felt the guilt start to sink in that she'd not only lied to Sarah about what happened, but she was going to back up that lie with a false report.

She had too many questions and needed answers.

Why did Amy say those names? Why was Jonas on that list? What happened to Adam Greber and Marie Deaver?

Now a new question popped up. Why was Detective Hicks so nice to Belinda and terrible with her? Could the cop think Rina was somehow involved in what happened with Adam Greber?

Rina shook her head. Why did she not say something about what Amy said to her in the gym instead of lying? Had she any common sense she would change her story now. Maybe Sarah would have some empathy. After all, one of the names the young woman mentioned was her husband.

Ex-husband, Rina reminded herself.

When Rina looked into Sarah's office with the report in her hand, she was on the phone. Sarah noticed her and waved her to come in. Rina looked at her falsified report and back to Sarah. She waved at Sarah and pointed at her watch as if she had to be somewhere. She took the report with her and left the ward and hurried to the main floor of the hospital.

Near the stairway was a nearly full trash can. She looked at the busy floor of people passing by, and quickly stuffed the report down into the trash. Once Rina was convinced her report was deep enough, she dug out her hand, making a face when she brushed against something sticky.

As Rina stormed down the hall she spotted Ron Alder talking to another member of hospital management. Ron wore a pinstripe suit and was holding a brown leather suitcase.

"Rina," he called out to her. She stopped while he shook the hand of the man he was talking to and walked up to her, taking his time to fix his suit as he did.

"Good morning," he said in his stern voice. "I understand there was an incident yesterday." He appeared upset. Rina wondered what Sarah had told him. She wondered if management was worried about what Phyllis Deaver would do in response.

"You heard about Amy Deaver?" Rina asked, surprised.

Suddenly the man's face softened. It was as if someone had told him someone he cared for had died. "What happened to Deaver's niece?" he asked.

"Nothing really," Rina lied. "There was another outage last night from the storm and Amy got out of her room. Security found her pretty quickly."

"Good. So the girl wasn't hurt? She didn't say anything?"

"Nothing." She stared at Ron, trying to keep it together. Amy had in fact said something. A list of names, including Ron Alder himself.

"I couldn't tell you what would happen if Deaver's niece managed to get hurt on your ward. You work mostly at midnight I hear, right?"

Rina nodded, taken aback that he knew anything about her or the ward. She wasn't entirely sure what Ron's role was at Holy Saints besides being part of management. She didn't believe it had anything to do with operations on the ward, though.

"Make sure you keep a good eye at night. If anything happens to that girl, it could mean trouble from Phyllis Deaver. I don't have to tell you what that means."

"How well do you know Amy Deaver?" Rina blurted out.

Ron looked at her. "She's Phyllis Deaver's' niece. What else is there to know? That wasn't what I wanted to talk to you about. My son, Cody, said you had a conversation with him yesterday. A frank one."

She had almost forgot about the altercation with Cody. "That's right, I did." Rina said.

"I need to apologize—"

Rina smiled. "You don't need to apologize for your son. He —"

Ron waved her off. "I mean apologize that I didn't make this clearer to you before. Let us be frank as well. I've read your most recent performance review. I know things aren't going well for you right now."

Rina furrowed her eyebrows. "What are you saying?"

"I'm saying you're doing a poor job, Dr. Kent. It's on your employee profile. Dr. Alloy has clearly said, without plainly stating it, how concerned she is. Now, I don't have to tell you how big mental health is becoming for hospitals. It's going to be the biggest money maker soon. That's why the next Holy Saints will be triple the size of the current one. Now, we need good people working those wards. We need to ensure the community knows how... professional the staff on ward are." Ron Alder took a step closer to Rina. "Now, play well in the sandbox with others, or else."

He took a step back again and smiled. "Was a pleasure catching up with you," he said loudly. He grabbed Rina's hand and shook it. "Remember my advice." He grabbed his luggage and headed down the hall without saying another word, his dress shoes clicking with each step. He didn't even look back to see if Rina was watching, which she was.

Rina took out her cell phone from her pocket. She dialed Jonas's number and waited.

"Rina?" he asked, surprised.

"Hey," she said back. "Are you still up for coffee?"

CHAPTER 14

Jonas waved to Rina when she stepped inside the busy coffee store outside the hospital. At his table he had two cups. Even though the cafeteria had its own coffee that many busy doctors, and nurses, and other staff would purchase, everyone knew if you wanted good java, you needed to cross the street outside to Green Cup.

The furniture was modern for a small coffee store. Personally, Rina always thought the furniture tried too hard to make the place more than what it was, being the best alternative to the worst coffee inside the hospital.

Jonas stood up as Rina approached the table. "Busy night?"

"Did you hear too?" Rina asked.

Jonas seemed confused. "Not sure what you mean."

Rina smiled. "Nothing. So, how are you?" Rina had to bite her tongue from demanding he answer all the questions she had in her head.

"Good, good." Jonas smiled back. "How's Denzel?"

"Same. I wanted to apologize about our last conversation. If you want, you could come by and have Denzel for a day or something. He would love it."

"Thanks. I miss the pup. Well, I guess he's not much of a pup now."

"He's getting big for sure. Soon he will be walking me." Rina laughed. When Jonas bought Denzel as a puppy, the breeder had lied to him saying he was a toy poodle. He was supposed to be one of those dogs you could carry in a handbag everywhere, but he kept growing, and the breeders lie becoming more evident. "Both of us are doctors and we didn't think to research better when we got Denzel."

When Rina said the word "us", Jonas's smile widened.

He sat upright in his chair. "Well, I suppose I wanted to talk more about us, in a safe place for *us.*" He looked around the coffee shop, and nudged the extra cup towards her. "I got you a large, one cream as well."

"Thanks," Rina said. "What did you want to say?"

Jonas lowered his head. "The best times of my life were with you. I know I messed up; I screwed everything for us. I have to make sure, though, and I won't give up until I know for sure... can there still be hope for us?"

"Jonas," Rina said softly.

"Listen," he said, holding her hand. "You coming here today tells me a lot. It tells me there's a chance. Do you see them?" Jonas nodded towards the corner of the cafeteria. An elderly couple were smiling at a table together. The woman taking a bite of a bagel and the man drinking from his cup. The man had a tube from his nose connected to a tank below the table that was on wheels.

"Cancer," Jonas whispered. "Dr. Janson told me about him. They've been married for over fifty years. They are both in their eighties. It's all the staff on the cancer ward are talking about. Everyone is gushing over their marriage. The woman visits him every day, for almost the full day. She only wants to be with her husband. Dr. Janson tells me the man has no chance in hell of surviving. The wife knows her husband won't be here much longer. You wouldn't know it by watching them, would you?"

Rina looked at the sparkle in the elderly man's eye as he spoke to his wife. They were too far away to hear what they were saying. He didn't seem distraught. She wasn't crying waves of tears. They just sat at the table, drinking and eating and seemingly enjoying each other's company. Rina could understand why people on the ward talked about them. They looked like a charming couple. When you read a love story, and in the end, you find out the couple will live happily ever after, you never see what they look like when they are old, and still in love. Rina imagined, just as Jonas did, that this couple perfectly conceptualized what happily ever after meant.

"I took a vow to you on the day we married," he whispered. "I meant every word of it, back then. I was stupid. I kissed that girl. Worst, I did it in front of people we know. I was upset with you for being so... busy with work. I know you were hurt and should have been there for you, but I wasn't. I failed you. I don't want to ever do that again. I want us to look at each other like they do." He glanced back at the elderly couple. "There's no reason why it can't still work. I will do whatever I need to do. Whatever you want, I will do. Let me prove my vow to you."

Rina smiled and sipped her coffee, not sure what to say. She thought of what her mother told her. Find someone who'll never give up on you.

"I... need some time to think about this," she finally replied.

"Okay," Jonas said, understanding. "Take as much time as you need. Whenever you want to talk about it with me, I'm here."

Rina nodded. "I've been helping Belinda with Deaver's niece," she said, changing the subject.

Jonas took a sip of his coffee and raised an eyebrow. "Are you her assigned psychiatrist now?

"Just helping... if I can. You said you didn't know Amy before she came to the ER that night?"

Jonas took another sip. "Not really. I think sometimes I'd see her with Phyllis."

"What about her mother, Marie?"

"Same. Sometimes I'd see her with Phyllis. We didn't talk much. Why are you asking?"

Rina shook her head. "I'm just trying to figure out Amy more. I feel if I can understand her mother, maybe I can help her"

"Sad what happened. Marie is still missing, I hear. Phyllis told me she believes she's living somewhere in the Vancouver area. How could a woman leave her daughter that way? I don't understand."

"Would there be a reason why Amy would be upset with you or with anyone else at the hospital?"

Jonas put his mug on the table. "What kind of question is that? I don't know the girl. Why would you assume a girl I don't know is upset with me? Is that what she said? I thought I heard the girl didn't speak. She didn't speak to me at the ER."

"She doesn't speak. But—"

"And questions about Marie Deaver too? What do you think happened between me and Marie? I know I made a mistake with that nurse—"

"You can't even say her name now? Veronica, wasn't it?"

"Right. I know her name. I just— Listen, I didn't do anything with Marie Deaver, if that's what you're getting to. You should speak with her ex."

"Marie has an ex in town. Who?"

"Why does any of this matter to you?" Jonas asked.

"I just want to find out more about Amy. I want to help her." Rina was about to bark out that she wanted to know why the girl whispered Jonas's name.

"I know what you want. This is all about that girl, Jenny. If you can help Amy, you can let go of what happened with Jenny, right?" Jonas shook his head. "I thought for a moment you came here for me."

"I did come here for you," Rina said sternly. "You need to know—"

Jonas stood up from the table. "I can't do this now. I hope you think about what I said. I want to talk about us, not Amy Deaver, or Phyllis or Marie, or anyone else. I want to talk about us." Jonas headed towards the exit but stopped and turned back to Rina.

"Please, if I'm wrong about us, tell me. Don't let me think we can still have something if there's no chance in hell of it happening. Do you hate me that much?"

"I don't hate you," Rina said, cradling her cup. "I want to know why..." She looked at Jonas but could feel his anger.

"Even now, after what I just said, you want to keep pressing me about this new patient of yours. I'm not sure what I'm doing to myself anymore." Jonas stormed out of the cafe, the door chiming loudly as he left. The elderly couple at the table stopped chatting to watch him leave before continuing with their conversation.

When Rina thought about the good times in her life, most of them included Jonas. He wasn't wrong. Rina wished she could forget everything that happened from the moment before Jenny Berange fell to her death in front of her. Jonas wished he could take back what he did.

She wished the same.

She wanted Jonas to look at her the same way he did when they were married. Sometimes she thought about what it would be like for her to come home not only to Denzel, but Jonas again.

But first she needed to know why his name was on her list.

CHAPTER 15

Almost immediately after Rina got home, she grabbed Denzel's leash. "Here boy!" she called, and her furry friend listened. He wagged his tail profusely as Rina connected the leash to his collar. "We're going to go for a long run today."

It was time to get some answers. Typically, she would try and sleep after work but there was no time for that. She had too many questions; none of them seemed connected but all of them seemed to go together.

Rina changed into her workout clothes and grabbed a few bottles of water for her and Denzel, putting them in a backpack. When she was prepared for her run, she took off from her doorstep. No warmup today. She needed to get to where she was going.

Adam Greber had been shot and killed in his home. Amy Deaver was admitted to Holy Saints psych ward soon after. Marie Deaver has been missing for over a month. Marie Deaver was herself a patient at Holy Saints psych ward under Adam Greber.

Amy Deaver gave Rina a list of names. Everyone she said worked or had worked at Holy Saints. The first being Adam Greber, now murdered. The last of Amy Deaver's names was Jonas.

Everything seemed too coincidental not to be connected.

Rina should have told Sarah the truth of what happened during the early morning hours with Amy. When she approached Jonas to get more answers, she only received more questions.

Who was Marie dating before she vanished? Why did people believe Marie was in Vancouver?

Rina continued to run with Denzel by her side. When she noticed his tongue hanging further out of his mouth than usual, she stopped to give him water, and herself a breath. She wasn't far now. Rina wasn't quite sure what she would do when she got to Phyllis Deaver's home. Phyllis was at the hospital and wouldn't be there, she knew. That hadn't stopped Rina from running to her beach house today.

Rina had to know what was happening. Phyllis Deaver was one of the names Amy said. What did it mean? Why didn't she just go to the cops and tell them?

Rina continued her run instead of coming up with a reasonable answer. Detective Hicks already seemed to have it in for her. What would happen if she went and told the cop the story of what had happened, especially after lying to Sarah?

Her job would be the least she would lose.

She finally reached the white picket fence of Phyllis Deaver's property. The fence encompassed a large field with a white house in the center. Along the white picket fence were signs warning that it was private property. Another mentioned that there were dogs, which Rina knew to be a lie.

In the distance beyond the house was a small beachfront and a dock with a canoe rocking in the waves against it. Rina noticed how fast the river was flowing and wondered if anyone on this beach could enjoy it.

She peered into the open areas of the home, seeing no signs of someone being inside or any activity. A car passed by, and Rina jumped.

Now what? Rina thought to herself. She considered knocking on the door first. Looking like someone just visiting. There were only two other homes on the block, spaced far apart from each other. She could brazenly walk up to all the doors and windows and test if any were open. She looked down at Denzel, who sat, staring at her, his tail wiggling against the concrete. Rina sighed.

She hadn't thought this out very well. What would she do with Denzel as she attempted all of this?

Another car drove past and came to a sudden stop in front of her. She saw Phyllis Deaver staring at her inside the vehicle, an eyebrow raised. She rolled a window down slowly.

"What are you doing out here?" she asked. "Did you run from your home? That's one hell of a workout."

Rina felt panicked and her heart was racing. "Real hard run today," she said, taking in deep breaths.

Phyllis smiled. "How about you come inside. My home is the large one behind you. I wanted to talk to you about Amy." When she didn't answer, Phyllis continued, "Are you okay?"

"That sounds great," Rina said with a smile.

CHAPTER 16

Rina sat inside Phyllis's living room as she made tea and coffee. Phyllis offered some biscuits, but Rina declined. The home was as rustic inside as outside. The furniture had plastic covers that made an awkward squeak when Rina moved.

Phyllis had asked Rina to keep Denzel outside. She had a strict rule of no pets inside her home. Rina obliged, leaving a bowl of water outside for Denzel, chaining him to the wooden porch.

As Phyllis made their drinks, Rina stared at the nearly empty walls. In the center of the longest was a large brick fireplace. Beside it was a gold holder for a fire poker, which was empty. There was a certain coziness to the room, except the lack of decor. Above the fireplace was a large photo of two women sitting in a canoe. Rina instantly identified Phyllis as one of the women, and the canoe as the one she'd seen tied to the dock.

Rina stared at the other woman. She was beautiful but didn't share a resemblance to Phyllis. She wore an emerald green necklace. Rina smiled. it was almost as if she was looking at a doppelganger of herself. Despite that, Rina knew she was staring at Marie Deaver.

On the mantle beneath the picture was a folded black letter. It reminded Rina of her home growing up. Her mother would place Christmas cards above the fire mantle. Rina peeked at the inside of the letter. "I crave your body, Phyllis," it read. Rina turned and smiled. It certainly wasn't a Christmas card.

Phyllis came into the living room with two mugs, placing

one in front of the table. Rina immediately sat on the chair and hoped Phyllis hadn't caught her snooping. "Thanks," she said, grabbing her cup and blowing away its steam. "That picture, is that Marie?"

Phyllis nodded. "That's her alright. My young sister. Pain in the ass since birth!" Rina moved on the couch, her bottom squeaking on her plastic.

"Sorry," she said. "I didn't mean to upset you."

"I'm not upset. So," she said, getting to the point, "I heard about Amy last night. How could something like that happen? You worked last night, right? Why didn't someone see my eighteen-year-old niece leaving the ward? She could have been hurt."

Rina was caught off guard, nearly spilling her tea on the plastic cover. Thankfully she managed not to make a mess. She could only imagine how Phyllis would react if she had.

"The building's terrible. The storm took out the power."

"I heard that. Still, you and the nurses on staff. Security. Nobody saw a girl leaving?"

When Phyllis had asked her to come inside her home, Rina had expected a much better experience. It was almost as if she had been tricked to come inside to get ambushed with questions. She should have known better.

Rina took a sip of tea before answering. "I shouldn't tell you this and promise me you won't say anything." Rina waited for Phyllis to nod before continuing, "I caught the security guard sleeping on the shift before the lights went out. I told Sarah about it. Apparently, it's not the first time it's happened."

"Ryan is his name, right?" she asked. "Damn that lanky piece of trash. Sarah will get it from me, believe me. I won't say anything that you've told me, but I was planning on giving it to her and your department either way."

"Understandable."

"I understand they are releasing Amy soon. Tomorrow or the day after. How can they do that?"

"I think you should talk to Belinda about that. I'm—"

"Not her primary psychiatrist, I know."

"Well, Belinda and Sarah make their calls on how to handle patient care. I can give you some good resources for outpatient care but I'm sure Sarah will give the same info to you too. I'm trying to help Belinda, though. I took a look at her notes last night on Amy's file."

"And what do you think? How can you help?"

"I was hoping I could look at her bedroom. I understand she and your sister were staying here."

"Living here is more like it. I've been taking care of my little sister and my niece for nearly a decade. That's right... Do you usually look into patients' bedrooms as a part of their clinical care?" Phyllis snapped.

"No, but I think it could help with Amy. Belinda is running out of ideas for how to treat her."

Phyllis scoffed. "Mental health treatment. Sometimes I feel like your field makes things up as you go."

"I'm just here to help," Rina said with a smile.

Phyllis smirked. "Well, follow me." She put her tea on the table and went down a hall. Rina quickly followed her. Phyllis went around a corner, opening a crooked door and pulling on a chain illuminating stairs going down to the basement.

"My sister and Amy stayed down here," Phyllis said. She started to go down the stairs, each step making a different squeak. The ceiling of the basement was low, and the carpet had a dank smell as if it had been flooded at some point. As they went further into the basement, Rina wondered why Phyllis had made her sister stay in the basement when there were multiple rooms on the main floor.

"I had some water damage back in 2013," Phyllis confirmed. "My sister hated the smell, but I gave her a rent-free room for her and my niece, so who was she to complain? This is Amy's room." She pointed across the hall. "That was Marie's."

Phyllis opened Amy's door. "Have a good look," she said. "Not much to look at though. My niece isn't the decorating type."

Phyllis wasn't kidding. The walls were bare except for a

Justin Bieber poster on the wall beside the bed. The odor in the bedroom was ten times worse than the hallway. She wondered how Marie and Amy could live in the basement in these conditions.

Across the room was a shelf full of books and puzzles. Rina stood in front of it, taking in its contents. Rows of puzzles took up most of the space. There was a box full of markers and construction paper.

"How long was your sister living with you?" Rina asked as she looked at the bare room.

"A little over nine years. All of them were rent-free, not that she would say thank you, ever."

"You're upset with your sister?"

Phyllis smirked. "Dr. Kent, please don't psychoanalyze me. First off, nobody wants to enter my mind, and second, I'm an open book, just ask. In fact, I'll just tell you. I was the oldest in my family. Marie, the baby. We didn't have it easy in our home. We were broke. I'm talking less than white trash. Still, I made something of myself. Marie coasted by. She got knocked up by some stranger she met at a bar. And who took care of that child? Me. Who paid all the bills to give them a life? Me. What thanks do I get? She leaves me her daughter to care for while she's off doing whatever she wants."

Rina opened a drawer beside Amy's bed and sighed when it was empty. "I heard she's in Vancouver."

Phyllis scoffed. "Who told you that?"

Rina looked at her. "Sorry, I didn't mean to offend you. It was Jonas."

"Your ex likes to spread gossip now? The police think she's in the city. They closed her case when they found some transactions made from her debit card there a week after she left."

"Has she made any more transactions?"

"I don't know. The police closed her file. She isn't missing. She just doesn't want to be found." Phyllis shook her head. "The only redeemable aspect of my sister was Amy, and she just up and leaves her."

"Would it be possible for me to see her bedroom too?" Rina asked, looking at the closed door across the hall.

"Now why would you want to do that?"

Rina waved around the room. "I'm not getting much from Amy's room. Maybe I can get more from Marie's."

"I'm not really comfortable with that."

Rina looked back at the shelf. Stuck between two puzzle boxes was a blue journal. The same type Amy would carry all the time. Rina was about to reach out for it when Phyllis tapped her on the shoulder.

"I'm not really comfortable with you being in this room either," she said. "So I think the tour of my home is over now."

The sound of Denzel barking broke the tension. Phyllis looked at her watch, and out into the hallway. "Dogs and the damn mailman." While she was distracted, Rina quickly grabbed the journal and stuffed it into her oversized sweater. She reached back and fixed the puzzle boxes on the shelf.

"I have the exact puzzle at my house," she said, touching a dolphin one. "Amy and her puzzles." She smiled at Phyllis, who didn't seem too impressed. "Thanks for showing me her room. I was hoping to get something out of this, but I guess I was wrong. Sorry to bother you." Phyllis didn't reply. She turned and started to walk towards the stairs.

"One last question for you," Rina said. "Jonas told me Marie was dating someone before she left. Do you know who it was?"

Phyllis turned to her and grimaced. "This is why I didn't want to tell anyone in this damn town a thing. Now everyone is snooping into my life and my sister's. What, are you a detective now, Rina? You going to find my sister and drag her back to Carrington? Please do, Detective Kent. Would make my day. Now why do you want to know who was dating my sister?"

"I'm hoping I can get in contact with Marie somehow. Maybe we can let her know what's happened with her daughter. Maybe she would come back in an instant if she knew what her daughter attempted to do."

Phyllis face fell immediately. All the lines of anger vanished. "I've been by myself with Amy for a little while now, angry at my sister for what she'd done. I've been getting used to taking care of the girl. I sometimes forget I'm not her mother. Marie would be devastated to know what Amy tried to do. I doubt her piece of garbage ex-boyfriend would be any help. I've pressed him before on the subject. I don't believe he knows anything useful. But you can try for yourself. Ron. Ronald Alder."

"From the hospital?"

Phyllis smiled. "He doesn't seem like the loving type, I know. Marie probably thought the man was her money ticket, but it ended just as quickly and explosively as it started."

"What happened? Why did they break up?"

"About a week before my sister left, they got into a huge fight in front of a dinner party at a fundraiser event. I'm not sure what it was about. Marie wouldn't tell me. Maybe you should ask Jonas since he seems to know all the gossip around town. I was happy when they broke up."

"Why?"

"Ron Alder's a piece of garbage? His son too, the nurse you work with. What's his name?"

"Cody," Rina answered. She certainly agreed with Phyllis about the son.

"That's the boy. I know young men try and get what they can get, but I caught him a few times trying to sweet talk Amy." Phyllis laughed. "What a stupid young man. He probably thought she was an easy target."

"Do you think Ron Alder had something to do with your sister leaving?"

"I don't know," Phyllis said. "It happened soon after they broke up. She took the end of that relationship hard. Part of me thinks he paid her off to keep her away from him. Maybe that's how she had enough money to get out of Carrington to begin with. To think," Phyllis said shaking her head, "my sister, all she ever talked about was getting enough money for Amy. She wanted her to live in her own apartment. There's a special program in Vancouver, where if you can afford it, staff take care of adults with intellectual disabilities. She would show me pamphlets and their website. With all the money she saved from being rent-free for years you think she would have some saved, maybe even try and get Amy into that program. Instead, she goes to Vancouver herself, with whatever money she has, and leaves her daughter... It gets me heated when I think about."

"You have a right to be angry. What was the name of the charity?"

"Community Developments for People with Intellectual Disabilities. CDPID."

Rina nodded. "Thanks for letting me in, Phyllis, and chatting with me about Amy." Rina walked past her, attempting her best to suck in her already petite gut to keep the journal hidden. Rina stared further into the dimly lit basement and saw a red light.

"I have a security system that runs twenty-four-seven," Phyllis said. "Flood lights line the fence and near the beach. Someone tried to break in a few months back. I had a hard time sleeping until I had it installed."

"That's scary," Rina said, attempting to move the journal in her sweater to conceal it better from the camera. She started up the stairs.

Phyllis didn't follow. "Is that why you came by? Was it coincidental you were running by my home?"

Rina took another two steps before stopping. She would have to give a reason. She turned and looked down at Phyllis. "After what happened last night with Amy, it made me think a lot about your niece. I was hoping to get some more ideas of how to help her. I guess I did run by here hoping you would be home."

"You know the pedia clinic closes at five," Phyllis said with a smirk. "You should have known I wouldn't have been home."

Rina gave a thin smile. "I'm running on fumes here. It's been over twenty hours and I haven't slept at all. After what happened with Adam, I've been having trouble sleeping. I'm not thinking all that well to be honest."

"That makes sense. You two must have been close. Did you talk to that detective? Hikers… or something like that?"

"Detective Hicks. Yeah, he came by last night."

"What a total piece of garbage of a cop, am I right?"

Rina smiled and agreed. She went up the stairs, and thanked Phyllis again before heading out the front door and grabbing Denzel. As soon as she untied his leash from a porch column, she immediately began running down the road. When she felt she was far enough, she took out the journal from underneath her sweater and skimmed the first few pages.

Amy had used multiple colored pens when writing in it. On the first page written in green was a sentence that asked what all provinces and territories in Canada were. Below it, written in blue in different handwriting, was a list of all of them. Two people had written in the book. One she assumed was Amy. She turned the page and there was another question written in green again.

"Name every prime minister of Canada." Below the question, Amy had answered in blue. Rina was foggy on her politics but many of the names she remembered. They appeared to be in historical order from what Rina could tell.

Phyllis had mentioned Marie homeschooled Amy. Had Rina stolen Amy's workbook? She shook her head at how embarrassed she was at the idea.

Strangely, some of the lower-case letters had been written backwards by Amy. Rina went through multiple pages and saw it over and over.

She flicked through the pages until she got to one written entirely in green. It read:

"Amy, always know that your mother loves you. I will do anything to make sure you have a better life than I had. I will do anything to protect you.

No matter what happens, always know that everything I

do, I do for you.

No matter what happens, never say a word."

Rina smiled. From now until work she would crack open a bottle of wine and read a teenage girl's journal.

CHAPTER 17

Nothing.

Rina had spent several hours reading the journal over several times. There was nothing that would help her understand what was happening. Marie had asked questions in green. Amy answered them, perfectly, in blue. The only entry that appeared to matter was the last one where Marie told Amy not to say a word.

If only her mother knew how well Amy was doing with that.

"Nothing" wasn't completely true, though. Written in green were the words to the song that had been driving Rina crazy, the one Amy had been humming the entire time at Holy Saints.

Rina sang the song in her room, as she read the words.

"Ladybird, ladybird, fly away home.

Your house is on fire and your children are gone.

All except one, and her name is Amy.

And she crept under the frying pan."

Rina had to google the lyrics because it didn't sound right. The name in the original song was Anne, but Marie had changed it to Amy. Rina read the lyrics in the workbook again, thinking of Amy. The lyrics crept her out. Many nursery rhymes' words seemed odd when you read them, but this song was worse.

Below the lyrics, written in blue, Amy had written the lyrics again, this time replacing her name with Mommy.

Rina thought and thought about what to do next. She lay on one side of the bed while Denzel plopped himself on the other side.

"I have to talk to Ronald Alder," she said out loud. Rina looked at her watch and saw she only had thirty minutes before work. She wouldn't have time to go to his home. She didn't even know where Ron lived anyway. That would be another problem to solve. There was a good chance that he was at the hospital. It wasn't unheard of to see someone from hospital management around when she started her shift.

She could get lucky and see him in his office. She could potentially even ask his son for his address, although that would be the absolute worst case.

Rina thought about how best to handle the situation on her drive to Holy Saints, still unsure what to do when she parked in the lot. Rina stepped out of her car and headed towards the staff entrance, taking a moment to glance at the fourth-floor window.

All Rina knew was she had to figure out what was happening soon, or come clean to Sarah, and potentially Detective Hicks, on the names Amy had told her. Before that, she would speak with Ron, and try and talk to Jonas one last time.

Rina went past security on the main floor saying she had to talk to Mr. Alder. They let her past, saying he was still in. She walked down the long hallway of offices until she found his name on a closed door. She knocked loudly but didn't hear a sound.

She knocked again. Hadn't the security guard said Ron was in? She put her ear against the door and heard footsteps on the other side. She knocked one last time.

The door opened partially, and Cody slid his head out and stared at her blankly.

"What do you want?" he asked.

Rina was surprised but looked at the name on the office door. "Your father. I was looking for him."

The nurse scoffed. "He's not here. He went home. It's late."

"Security said he was still in."

"Security made a mistake," Cody said coldly. "Everyone

makes mistakes, Dr. Kent. Why do you need my father?"

"Can I have his number?" she asked.

Cody furrowed his brow. "Can you just leave me alone? I'm putting in to move my shift away from yours as much as possible. My father says I should make an official complaint about you, you know."

Rina shook her head. "Listen, this is not about that. I couldn't care less right now. I just need to speak to your dad."

"About what?"

"That's between him and me. Can you give me his number now?"

"No, but give me yours and I'll text him. If he wants to call you back tonight, it's up to him, if not, not my problem."

"That's okay. Just let him know that I came by, please. Do you always hang out in your father's office when he's not around?"

Cody didn't answer, closing the door with force.

Rina could feel her blood rising just talking to him again. She hoped he'd follow through with changing shift rotations to avoid working with her. It would make her nights much better not having some boyish nurse attempting, poorly, to flirt with her.

Rina went up the elevator to the fourth floor, happy that it was operational again. She smiled and waved at Ryan the security guard as she used her pass to enter. For a change, the guard did not look at her or acknowledge her presence. The ward doors opened, and Ryan turned to her.

"I wasn't sleeping," he said under his breath. "That's what you told them. You insinuated that I was negligent."

"Well, you were when I went into the changing room."

Ryan didn't respond immediately. "I wasn't sleeping when the power went out. I have a protocol. I go down the hall to make sure all the emergency lighting is on. I go into the wards to make sure as well. The girl must have split when I was doing my checks. The doors aren't functioning correctly when the power is working. I wasn't aware that it wasn't locked. I wasn't sleeping. I was doing my job."

"I'm sorry," Rina said. "I understand it can be difficult at times to stay alert in your job. I did catch you sleeping before. These patients' safety is your responsibility. Next time you need a break to freshen up, grab a coffee, let me know. I can help. And I'll let Dr. Alloy know we talked, okay?"

"That works. Thanks."

Rina entered the ward. Nurse Bethany was finishing off giving night meds and some patients were already going to their rooms for the night. She spotted Amy immediately in her usual spot with a puzzle. Rina wondered how many times she had done the same puzzle since coming to the ward.

Belinda approached Rina with a large smile. "Evening."

"Hey," Rina said back. She nodded towards Amy. "Anything new with our favourite patient?"

"Just an upcoming discharge date. What else can we do? She seems stable enough. We'll—"

"Create a safety plan for her and Phyllis," Rina interjected. Belinda nodded. "Is Sarah still here?"

Belinda shook her head. "Not tonight. She had to leave early, she said. Some personal matters. Personally, I think she's having a hard time over Adam." Belinda let out a heavy breath. "I know I was emotional too yesterday, but Sarah has been worse. I catch her wiping away tears when she thinks no one is watching."

Rina lowered her head. "Maybe she needs help."

Belinda gave a thin smile. "Don't we all? Let's get patient reviews over with," she said, pointing towards her office. "I just want to go home, put on a movie and do nothing for the rest of the night."

After their meeting, Dr. Knowles left in a hurry. As usual, the rec room was near empty when Rina went back to check, except for Amy. She appeared to be the last to go to her room, and needed several prompts to leave her seat, and her puzzle. Bethany was already attempting to get Amy to stand.

"Let's go, young lady," she barked. "Nighttime. Clean up

the puzzle. Put it back on the shelf. Let's go."

Rina stepped beside her. "It's okay, Bethany. Let me talk to her for a moment. I'll get her ready for the night."

Bethany shook her head. "Okay, Dr. Kent."

Rina looked at Amy, who didn't look back. She remained focused on the puzzle, her journal under her armpit. Rina grabbed a chair and sat on the other side of the table.

"Good evening, Amy," she said with a thin smile. Amy didn't respond. Rina glanced down at the puzzle, which was nearly complete. Amy continued to put the pieces in their proper spots. After a moment, Amy hummed her song and rocked in her chair.

Rina smiled. "Ladybird, Ladybird. Fly away home." Amy looked up at her, confused. "Your house is on fire, and your children are gone. All except Amy... Did your mom sing it to you often?"

Amy lowered her head and continued to put the pieces into place. For a moment, Rina thought she saw her frowning.

"You don't like to talk about Mom?" Rina asked.

Amy didn't answer. She was down to one last piece, but it was missing. Amy looked around the table and at her feet. The girl seemed almost frantic.

Rina looked down and saw a small, half torn puzzle piece on the floor. "I think this is what you need," she said, grabbing it and giving it to her. Amy smiled and completed the puzzle. She immediately broke the puzzle into pieces and began putting them into the box.

"Why did you say their names?" Rina asked. "I need to know. Jonas, he's my husband. My ex-husband, actually."

Amy looked up at her, her face stoic. She shook her head and continued to put the pieces away.

"I need to know, Amy. I know you can speak. You said their names. You said Adam Greber's name too. He's dead, did you know that? I'm not trying to scare you, but I need to know what's happening." Amy continued to ignore her. Rina could feel her hand gripping tight at her side. "I need to know, Amy. I will have to tell the cops what you told me."

Amy put the last few pieces of the puzzle away and stood up from the table. Rina reached out and grabbed her arm.

"Don't say a word," Rina said. Amy attempted to pull her arm away and Rina let go immediately. "Your mom told you the same." Rina folded her white jacket, revealing the journal she'd concealed. "This is your journal, Amy. Why did your mom tell you not to say a word? What happened? I need to know!"

"Easy, Dr. Kent," Bethany said. Rina turned to the nurse and tried to compose herself, hiding the journal. "They say I'm the harsh one." Bethany laughed.

Rina stood up from table and hurried down the hallway to her office.

CHAPTER 18

Rina sat in her office, twirling her hair. She used to do it as a child. It was one of those habits that she knew was for comfort but couldn't stop. The nursery rhyme Marie sang to her daughter was now thoroughly stuck in her mind.

Rina was embarrassed and unsure what to do. How could she have made a scene like that in front of Nurse Bethany? She needed answers, though. Amy wasn't going to tell her them.

Somehow, she knew that Amy's other journal, the one she carried with her everywhere, wasn't full of Canadian geography. Rina had to see what was inside.

Would Amy ever let her look, though? Rina knew the answer to that question.

Could she somehow connect with her in a way that Amy would start to open up, and allow her to look?

Rina reminded herself that the last part of the journal read "don't say a word".

What did it all mean? How could she find out?

She reached into her pocket and grabbed her cell and texted Jonas.

"Can we talk? Meet for coffee again? I need to speak to you about something."

Rina waited for him to read the message. She stared at her text, waiting for the symbol to pop up beside it that said the text had been seen. Instead, nothing happened but her staring at her phone.

Rina put it on the desk and sighed. She stared at her office computer, until she had another idea.

Just like Marie, Ron Alder would have medical records on file. Typically, those that worked at the hospital had their medical records sealed. Rina leaned towards her computer. Only one of Marie's records was private though. There could be a chance Ron's records weren't all private as well. She had to talk to him, and his records would have his address.

Rina opened the health records system and started to type in his name in the search bar, but didn't hit enter. Her computer, just as all systems in the hospital, was monitored. What if someone from the IT department flagged her search for Ronald Alder? What possible explanation could she have for searching for his name? He worked in management, and already wanted her job for what happened with Cody. How many ethical standards was she willing to break?

Rina leaned back in her chair. How deep in trouble was she willing to get into? She looked at her cell and was happy to see she had a new message.

She was even more excited when she saw it was from Jonas.

"Hey, I can't tonight. Poker night at Caleb Janson's, remember? He still has his weekly game. Even though he can't bluff to save his life, he still likes hosting for everyone to come. What about tomorrow? I work during the day but maybe we can meet up later. For dinner?"

Rina smiled. She wasn't sure why it made her happy. Find someone who'll never give up on you. If she asked her mother what to do with Jonas she wondered what she would say? It felt good how Jonas continued to pursue her. She planned on telling him everything she'd learned. She needed to get everything off her chest.

"Dinner sounds great," she wrote back. "See you at five?"

He responded immediately. "That sounds great. What about Giovanni's?"

She smiled again. Some couples have certain things in common they enjoy doing. Some read together. Others exercise.

Jonas and Rina were foodies. They had visited every restaurant within twenty kilometers. They always found themselves going back to this small Italian restaurant in town. The pasta was made fresh there. The sauce was perfect. They both enjoyed the seafood.

"Or we could try a new place," Jonas texted.

Rina immediately replied. "No, let's meet at Giovanni's, like old times." Rina put her phone back into her pocket and stood from her desk, unable to hide her smile.

She thought of Amy again. She knew there must be a way to connect with her and just had to think harder. Belinda had attempted to connect with her using puzzles. Rina had tried something similar.

Suddenly it struck her. Helping Amy with puzzles failed, but what if you could communicate with her using a puzzle?

Rina opened a search bar and looked. It had to exist, she knew. She scrolled until she found the item. The price was extremely high, but if it could help it would be worth it. She purchased multiple boxes and requested express delivery. It would arrive tomorrow night, the invoice confirmed.

She stood up from her desk. She could be on to something, or it could be another flopped attempt. Belinda said she would be discharged soon, so Rina might as well try. She had likely another night with Amy to attempt it.

Rina walked down the dimly lit hall. She heard Bethany's distant footsteps.

"Dr. Kent," she called out.

"Hey, Bethany."

Her face was cold, as usual, but this time she had a scowl. "What was that before, with Amy Deaver?"

Rina feigned a smile. "Sometimes, when you try and try to connect with someone, to help them, and they give you nothing back, it can be hard, that's it."

She didn't seem to like the answer. "I shouldn't tell you this, but Dr. Alloy asked me to let her know if you did anything *funny*."

"Sarah said that to you?"

Bethany nodded. "I'm not sure what kind of mess you're in. You usually keep to yourself on your night shifts, and that's the way I like it. Go to work, come home, and repeat. I don't want trouble. I just want my paycheck. I won't tell her what I saw, but you need to get it together. Some of the other psychiatrists when they were on nights would make my life hell. More work. I like working with you. Now, I didn't say anything to you, right?"

"I won't say a word." Rina smiled. "Thanks. I'll keep that in mind."

"I'd start talking to my union rep too, if I were you."

"What about Cody Alder? Did he see what happened with Amy?"

Bethany shook her head. "He took a day off. Used a personal day."

"I just saw him."

"He said he wasn't feeling good today," she said with a scoff. "You ask me, he's scared of you." She laughed. "I heard what you said to him. These halls can echo at night. Good for you. That brat is always wandering around with his penis leading the way. I even caught him talking funny to that girl, Amy."

"What did he say?" Rina asked.

"Something about going somewhere when she's discharged. Some park. I couldn't hear everything, but it didn't sound right. Anyway, I saw how you handled that brat and put him in his place. I like that about you." Bethany mentioned she had to get caught up with some reporting and walked off to the nurse's shared office.

Rina continued towards the patients' rooms. She knew Sarah Alloy was worried about how she was doing. She wouldn't think she would go to an extreme like asking Bethany to watch her.

When she came to Amy's door, Rina opened the slot and saw she was sleeping. Rina wondered how the girl could sleep with such inactivity all day. Despite her thoughts, Amy looked knocked out, and she could hear the faint sounds of her heavy breathing.

Rina looked around the hall, confirming no one was around but her. She opened Amy's bedroom door. Thankfully, the door creak was at an all-time low.

Rina took her time creeping inside, ensuring with each step that Amy was still sleeping. Amy laid in a fetal position; the journal wrapped loosely in her hand. The edge of the book almost looked like it could teeter off her fingers and onto the floor.

Rina took her time grabbing the side of the book and pulling it slowly from Amy's hand. Rina was now kneeling beside the bed and could feel Amy' breath against her arm. She tried to calm herself, Amy's deep breathing helping her do so.

Finally, the book was completely off the bed and in Rina's hands. She opened the first page, pursing her lips when she saw what was inside. It was Amy's writing. She could tell from the backwards As. In large letters across the page, Amy had written: Adam Greber, Ron Alder, Phyllis Deaver, Jonas Kent.

The names took up the full page. Rina turned to the second page.

"Don't say a word," it read.

The third page was the list of names again, followed by "don't say a word" at the bottom.

The fourth page had one written name: "Adam Greber." The next page: "Ron Alder." She turned the page and saw "Phyllis Deaver". Lastly, it read "Jonas Kent". The page after read, "Don't say a word." She flicked through the rest of the journal, but it was just the list of names. Sometimes the names were in the same order, other times random.

In her frustration, Rina hadn't realized Amy's heavy breathing had stopped. Rina lowered the journal and Amy stared back at her.

Her young eyes stared directly at Rina. Her eyebrows furrowed. Rina placed the journal on the bed. Amy sat up and grabbed her book, holding it tightly.

"Don't say a word," Rina whispered.

"What are you doing?" Rina turned to see Bethany looking at her. Her arms were folded.

"Wellness check," Rina answered. "I opened the slot and saw she had something in her hand. I was worried."

"Her journal?" the nurse said. "Okay, Amy, time for sleep."

Rina nodded. "Good idea." She turned to Amy. "Goodnight." Amy watched until Rina was out of the room and closed the door behind her.

"What did I just say?" Bethany said. "Did we not just talk about this?"

"I was just doing a wellness check," Rina said.

"Tell it to Dr. Alloy. I'm not a rat, but you can't do stuff that will get me in trouble."

"That's fine," Rina said. "I wasn't doing anything wrong. You don't have to worry."

Rina stormed down the hall until she was near her office. She looked back and saw Bethany still staring at her. Rina shut the door behind her and sat at her desk again.

The names. Each of them continuously scribbled in the journal. Rina could feel her heart racing. What was happening? All the lies she had told to conceal what Amy said. What would happen if everything came out and people found out?

She still needed answers. Ron Alder could have them. Rina had *dirt* on his son. She could talk to him in exchange for a promise to "play nicely in the sandbox" with Cody from now on.

Rina opened the computer and searched for his name. Luckily, Ron had several medical records on file. Two of them were blanked off, and she couldn't access them. She clicked on the most recent medical record. It was a visit to the stress test center at the hospital for high blood pressure. The tests showed that he had slightly higher BP than others at his age. It was recommended that he maintain a better diet, exercise and attempt medication in three months if nothing changed.

None of that mattered to Rina, except for the box of info at the top. Patient's address: 1545 Rosewind Street.

Rina looked at the time. It was only a little after ten at night. Late for a visit with a co-worker, but not late enough to not get answers.

Rina left her office, listening for the footsteps of anyone nearby. She hurried down the hall and swiped her pass at the entrance. When the light turned green, she opened the door and waved at Ryan.

"Hey, Ryan," she said sweetly. "I forgot some important files at home. I have to finish a report before the end of my shift though and need them. I'll just be off site no longer than an hour." Ryan smiled, alert, with a cup of coffee in his hand.

CHAPTER 19

At 1545 Rosewind Street, the killer waited patiently for Ron Alder to return home. They knew it could be some time before he arrived given the late hours he sometimes put in, but were willing to wait as long as needed.

When Ron opened the front door, he immediately put his briefcase beside it, and went upstairs to his bedroom. The killer had waited in the living room. Somehow Ron walked past them in the dark, not noticing. The killer smiled and stood, and quietly followed him, checking their gun to ensure they were ready.

The killer tried their best to move swiftly without much noise but one stair creaked. They let out a heavy breath.

Ron Alder was not a retired man like Adam Greber. He could... fight back. There was a possibility that he owned guns himself. The killer had made careful plans, though. They'd searched the main bedroom, kitchen, bathroom, and anywhere else they knew Ron could get to if he attempted to put up a fight. The killer had found no weapons. Ron Alder was the type of man who could have a secret safe somewhere. The killer would make sure to watch him carefully.

The killer continued up the stairs, listening for where Ron was. When they reached the top of the stairs, they heard him in his bedroom. They peaked inside the open door to see him changing into silk white pajamas. Ron went to a nightstand beside his bed, filled a rock glass with scotch from a drink tray. He opened a small wooden box, taking out a thick cigar.

Ron grabbed a cigar cutter and cut off the tip of it, took a long sniff of it, and grabbed a matchbox from the nightstand. Ron Alder appeared to have a nightly routine he enjoyed coming home to.

The killer smiled, knowing they had ruined it. They knocked on the open door with one hand, concealing the gun in the other, making their presence known.

Ron jumped. "Jesus!" he yelled, dropping the cigar. "What the hell are you doing?"

This time the killer hadn't bothered with a mask. They would enjoy Ron's face when he realized why they were in his home. The killer knocked on the door again, this time with the gun.

"Good evening, Ronald," the killer said.

"What— why?"

"You know why," the killer said.

"After everything I did for you, you point that gun at me? So, it was you who killed Adam Greber? We hoped it was just an ex-patient, someone who had a problem with the old man. But you? We had a deal!"

"And you broke the deal," the killer barked. "Amy Deaver?"

"What about her?" Ron said. He grabbed his rock glass and took a sip. He bent over for his cigar but the killer tsked him and he straightened up.

The killer pointed the gun at his head. "Whose idea was it to try and kill her? The high dose of Tylenol and Advil you... injected her with."

Ron shook his head. "It wasn't my—"

"Who tried to kill her!"

"I didn't inject her," Ron said softly. "Please. We can work this out. It doesn't have to be like this. You can take the money. None of this matters, so long as the girl doesn't talk and Marie Deaver never comes back."

"I don't believe him," a third voice said. The killer's accomplice entered the room with a large knife they'd grabbed from the kitchen. They touched the tip of the knife with a finger, ensuring its sharpness.

Ron turned grey. "Oh god, no." He looked at the killer again. "You don't have to hurt me. We can work together, again."

"You didn't answer the question," the accomplice said sternly. "Who injected Amy to make it look like the girl tried to kill herself?"

"Greber!" Ron said promptly. "What do I know about overdosing? It was his idea!"

The killer laughed. "Dr. Greber wouldn't have the gall to try and kill Amy. He needed someone to rile him up enough to do it. I already know it was you."

"Oh god," Ron said, his hands shaking. He held them out towards the killer. "Don't I mean anything to you? You would do this to me? Please, don't."

The accomplice smiled. "This is a good look for you, Ronald. I like it. Beg some more for your life. Maybe we will like what you say."

"Please. You don't have to. We can work out a deal."

"Deal? We tried that once with you. You always like to pretend to be a powerful man. Management at the hospital. Looking down on everyone else."

"He's not a very good beggar," the accomplice agreed, raising the knife. "Should we give him another chance?"

"He has been useful," the killer said. "You need to confess, though. Say what you did."

Ron Alder lowered his head. He got down on his knees and reached up to the killer. "I... tried to get Greber to kill the girl when she was alone at home. He didn't give her enough. She lived. I'm glad she did. It was a huge mistake. Please, we can work this out. You can have whatever you want. Please. There's something you don't know. Everything is going to be out in the open soon. Please! Let me tell you what you don't know!"

The killer looked at the accomplice. "A little bit better, no? Your call. What do you want to do with him?"

CHAPTER 20

Rina knocked hard on Ron Alder's front door. She waited patiently for a response. After a few moments she rang the doorbell, and again knocked. Nobody answered.

Rina knew he was home. His black Escalade was parked in the driveway, clear as day. Not knowing what else she could do, she knocked again.

"Hell," Rina blurted out. "What now?" She looked at her watch; it was nearly ten thirty at night. Ron did not come off as the type to pass out at this time, but she could be wrong.

Rina returned to her car, but before getting inside she turned and looked at the home's large windows. She scanned each of them for movement.

A voice inside Rina told her to leave, but she needed to talk to Ron. Things were not adding up, and Rina had to know why. Everything stemmed from Amy Deaver, an eighteen-year-old autistic girl who tried to kill herself.

Ron Alder had answers.

Rina walked around the side of the house, opening a small black gate. She peered into the backyard and the rear windows. A light in an upstairs room caught her attention. Rina squinted and saw a shadow of something inside.

Could be a lamp or anything, she thought. Suddenly, the shadow moved.

"Hey!" Rina called. She ran to the front door and knocked and rang the doorbell again. She waited patiently for a response from Ron, who she'd clearly seen inside. He lived alone.

Divorced, his son did not live with him, although Rina was sure he wished he still could.

"C'mon!" Rina shouted again.

A snapping sound made her turn her head towards the driveway. All she saw was her car. She thought she heard footsteps and called out.

"Mr. Alder? I need to talk to you. It's not about Cody." She headed out to her car, but nobody was there. Despite not seeing anything, she had a strange feeling.

She knew someone was in the house. They weren't answering the door though. She looked up at the front windows again, hoping to see movement. They were dark. Nothing was visible.

"We need to talk!" Rina shouted. "Please!" When nothing happened, Rina got into her car, and started it. The lights turned on. She put her foot on the brake and looked at her rear-view mirror. The red brake lights illuminated a group of thick trees across the street. Rina backed up her car and started to leave the driveway. She looked again at the rear-view and for a moment thought she saw something move in the brush behind her.

"Just leave!" the voice inside her yelled. She had never experienced such a visceral feeling of danger before. This time she listened to her gut and began driving down the street. She looked out into the dark wooded area as she did.

When she got back to the hospital, she waved at Ryan before swiping her pass. "Still quiet?" she asked the guard.

"Nothing to report," Ryan said. "Where's your files?"

"What's that?" Rina asked.

"The files you went home to grab."

Rina shook her head. "What a night," she said, smiling. "I think I need more coffee too. They weren't at home. I think I left them in Dr. Knowles' office."

CHAPTER 21

Rina dreaded the remainder of her shift. Thankfully no further issues occurred. Bethany ignored Rina, which on midnights wasn't difficult to do. The patients woke up at their regular time. Amy sat at her table with her puzzle as usual. Rina greeted all the patients, talking to Amy last.

"Good morning, Amy," she said to the young woman. Amy didn't respond. Rina took that as a good sign. She worried the patient would start to yell at the sight of Rina over what happened in her room.

Soon after, Sarah entered and smiled at Rina, greeting her before going to her office. Rina spotted Bethany heading to her room and closing the door behind her. She tried to not show concern and continued her usual conversations she had with her patients and others at Holy Saints.

"Good morning," Belinda said, another expensive latte in her hand. "How did the night go?"

Rina was about to answer when Sarah came towards them. Typically, she had a calming walk, almost galivanting around the ward since being Chief of Psychiatry. Today she walked with purpose directly towards Rina.

"Rina," she said with a harsh tone, "can we talk in my office?" Belinda stared at Rina with a look of surprise.

"Of course, Sarah," she said.

"Can you shut the door?" Sarah asked once they were inside. Sarah sat behind her desk and Rina on the couch. "So, what happened last night? Bethany came to me this morning, concerned. She said you grabbed Amy Deaver's hand forcefully and at night went into her room. What's happening here, Rina?"

Rina lowered her head. "There's a lot going on, to be honest. I—"

Sarah cut her off. "You know, I had Ron Alder from management coming down here and asking about you too?"

"You saw Ron today?" she asked, surprised, but Sarah didn't answer.

"I asked you to complete a report on what happened with Amy, and you didn't. I... If something like this happens again, I'll have to write you up, or worse. I hate doing this, Rina, I do."

"Sarah," Rina pleaded. "Let me explain. A lot has been happening."

Sarah nodded. "I know, Rina. I asked you to take time off to get better. I may not be *asking* too much longer. I want you to go home. Think really hard about what you want. I want you to stay on the ward with us, I do. I know what you are capable of. I've seen it. What happened with that girl, Jenny, I took what you said to me at Adam Greber's party to heart. I had a hard time with you blaming me for what Jenny Berange did. I had a hard time because I blamed myself, before you ever did."

"If that table wasn't in the rec room, it wouldn't have happened."

"Here we go again. The blaming. That table shouldn't have been there, you're right. It took me some time to forgive myself for that mistake... What about you? I read the incident report you wrote on Jenny Berange. She approached you asking for help, and you left her alone. What would have happened if you reacted immediately to her? Should we blame you for what happened?"

Rina felt a tear forming and rolling down her cheek. "I— you shouldn't have— never mind. This is useless."

Sarah breathed out. "It is, Rina. That's the point. You and I both know as psychiatrists that Jenny Berange choosing to kill herself was neither of our faults. The difference is, you continue to internalize it as something you did wrong. You need to stop."

Rina felt her blood pressure rising. She wondered if she looked as red as she felt inside. She was about to say words to her boss that would certainly help Ron Alder get her fired.

"Is there anything else?" Rina asked.

"I'll see you tonight," Sarah said. Rina left the office. She gathered her things and left the ward, taking the elevator to the first floor. As she was about to leave, she spotted the security guard she'd seen near management's offices.

"Hey," she said to the guard. "Can I speak with Ron Alder? Is he in?"

The guard smiled and greeted Rina. "Sorry, I haven't seen him."

CHAPTER 22

Rina waved at Jonas when he entered the restaurant. He smiled when he saw her. He wore a black blazer over a white dress shirt and dark wash jeans. She had forgot how attractive he was. She had been so caught up being angry at him to see any of his good looks. She'd put some effort into her appearance as well, wearing a black dress that slimmed her figure, and red lipstick. It was a combination that Jonas had loved when they were married.

"You look... great," he said, taking a seat at the other side of the table.

"Thanks. Did you just get off work?"

"Yeah, it was a gruesome day. A paramedic brought in a man they had to perform an emergency tracheotomy on. It was botched, and we had to have Dr. Janson do emergency surgery, but the man lived. It was all because of what that paramedic did. Amazing. Then... sorry, I didn't want to talk about work with you. I told myself I wasn't going to do that this time."

"It's okay," Rina said. "It's what we are passionate about, helping people. I wanted to see you tonight for a few reasons—"

"Any drinks tonight?" the waiter interjected. "Would you like a wine list?"

Jonas glanced at Rina. "I think you're working in a few hours, right? We're okay for drinks, thank you." The waiter said he would bring water for them. Jonas turned to Rina. "What were you saying?"

Rina took in a deep breath. "Well, you and I – we like to

help others, that's why we do the work we do." Jonas nodded. Rina took her time trying to find the words. She didn't want to bring up Amy right away. She couldn't help it, though.

"It's about Deaver's niece again?" Jonas said with a shake of his head. "I won't get angry this time. What is it? I'm actually sorry for how I acted last time. I got defensive. I should have listened."

"I'm concerned for you," Rina said, forcing the words.

Jonas leaned back in his chair. "What do you mean?"

Out of nowhere, the waiter came back to the table with two cups of water. Rina waited for him to leave before continuing.

"Do we know what we will be having tonight?" the waiter asked.

"More time, please," Jonas said politely. The waiter bowed his head and left. "Why are you concerned for me?" he asked.

"I haven't been telling the truth about something that happened with Amy Deaver." Rina took a sip of water.

"Amy Deaver? What did she say I did?"

"So, last night, I was in the gym working out. Well, Amy managed to get into the gym where I was. Before security came to get her, she talked to me."

Jonas shifted in his chair. "What did she say? I don't understand what this has to do with me."

"She whispered a list of names to me," Rina said, looking around the restaurant.

"Would you like me to review our appetizers or main entrees?" the waiter said, appearing out of nowhere. "We have fine calamari with tomato sauce."

"More time," Rina and Jonas said almost in unison. The waiter immediately left, apologizing if he'd interrupted.

Rina took a sip of water before continuing. "She said the names Adam Greber, Ron Alder, Phyllis Deaver... and you."

"Me," Jonas said. "She just listed a bunch of names to you?"

Rina nodded. "Then she said, 'Don't say a word.'"

Jonas scratched his head, unsure what to say. "Don't say a word," he repeated.

"Her journal. She carries it everywhere with her. The other night, I snuck into her room and looked at it."

"You snuck in her room? Rina, what are you doing?"

She laughed. "Just wait until I tell you everything. Worse part was Bethany caught me going into Amy's room. Sarah really gave it to me this morning. Things are not good at work right now. So... I look at Amy's journal. On every page are the names of the people she told me. Every time, after the list, she writes—"

"Don't say a word," Jonas interrupted. "What do Sarah and Belinda think?"

"I haven't told them yet," Rina said, taking a deep breath.

"What? Why?"

"That night when Amy whispered your name with the others, it scared me. I don't know why, but I didn't tell anybody what she said. They still think she's completely mute."

"But why haven't you still not told anyone?"

"Adam Greber was one of those names. He's been murdered. When Amy was admitted at Holy Saints, he was murdered. He's the first name on the list."

Jonas shook his head. "Wait, what are you trying to say? You think Amy killed Adam Greber?"

"No, not her. I don't know who. It just doesn't make sense. You know Marie Deaver is missing, and at one time Marie was a patient on the psych ward as well."

Jonas took a sip of water, rubbing his head. "I don't get this. Adam Greber was murdered, and you think this eighteen-year-old patient has something to do with it?"

"He was one of the names she told me. One of the names in her book, and now he's dead."

Jonas smiled. "I... love you. I do. I worry about what goes on in your mind though, Rina. I only really know Amy from when she was my patient when she tried to kill herself, that's it. Why would I be on her list of names?"

"I don't know, but I'm worried," Rina said.

"Worried that something will happen to me, like Greber?"

"Yes, I guess. I need to know why your name would be on her list. I was hoping you could help me figure this out."

"I don't know," Jonas said. "Ron Alder, he dated Marie Deaver. I guess that could be a reason why he's on it. Adam Greber was Amy's mother psychiatrist at Holy Saints, I guess I could be on that list because Amy was my patient?" Jonas took a deep breath. "Something you really need to consider here too, is she's... not well. There could many reasons why she keeps a list of names. I'm disturbed to be on it, but what I'm saying is, she's sick. That's why she's on the ward to begin with. Rina, you want my advice? Tell Sarah and Belinda what Amy said to you. None of this makes sense. You're doing things that don't make sense. Now I'm worried about you." Jonas picked up his glass to take a drink.

"I stole Amy's journal from Phyllis's house," Rina blurted out.

Jonas spit out his water, using his napkin to quickly wipe up the mess on the table. "Come again?"

Rina laughed. "I'm telling you all of this, and I'm starting to feel very foolish. I don't know why I didn't just tell Sarah the truth about what happened with Amy."

"Whoa, can we backtrack a little." Jonas leaned towards her. "You broke into Phyllis Deaver's house and stole her niece's journal? What has happened to my wife?"

Rina squirmed in her chair. "Well..."

"Right... sorry. Sometimes I still say— never mind. But what are you doing?"

Rina laughed again. "I don't know. I didn't break into the house, though. I snatched it when she wasn't looking." She looked around the restaurant. "Where did that waiter go? Maybe I should have a glass of wine."

"What did Amy's other journal say?"

"Not much. It seemed to be a workbook for her homeschooling. On one page, though, was a message from her mother telling her that everything she has done, she did for

Amy. And then she told her to—"

"Not say a word," Jonas said again. "Right."

"I also went to Ron Alder's house in the middle of the night, trying to get answers."

Jonas covered his face. "Rina, you're going to get yourself fired. You're not a cop. Was Ron upset?"

"He was home," Rina said, "but he didn't answer the door."

"Do you blame him?" Jonas asked bluntly.

Rina nodded. "I guess not. I don't know what to do. I could let the cops know what I saw in the journal. Of course, that means dealing with Phyllis and telling her I stole it from her house." Rina covered her face now. "I've made a good mess of my life, it seems."

"Nothing that can't be undone," Jonas said. He reached into his pocket, grabbed his cell and dialled.

"Who are you calling?" Rina asked.

"Ron Alder."

Rina tried to grab his phone. "What are you doing, Jonas?"

Jonas put up a finger. "It's Jonas Kent. When you get this, please call me." He hung up his cell and smiled at Rina. "I'm going to smooth this over."

"I'm surprised you have his number."

"I purposefully make it a point to make good connections with management," Jonas said.

"There's more to this Ron Alder story, though. His son flirted with me at work. Continues to flirt with me at work. On numerous occasions. I called him out on it and Ron pulled me aside, and said I needed to stop making waves for his son, or else."

Jonas's smile vanished. "Or else... what? What did he say to you? What did his son say to you?"

"He indicated that when the time comes for us to transition to the new hospital, maybe I wouldn't be welcome."

Jonas nodded, his face flat. "And the son, what did he say to you?"

"Nothing, Jonas. I can handle myself. I shouldn't have said anything to you. I'm worried if you talk to him, he will bring it up and I wanted to tell you first. I'm fine."

"Okay," he said. "But promise me, no more of this. I'm safe. All the rest of the names you said are safe... and alive."

"Okay. But maybe I should call the police and tell them all of this."

Jonas shrugged. "I'm not sure what you would tell them that makes any sense."

"I do have another idea of how I can try and get answers from Amy," Rina said.

"She's still talking?"

"No, she hasn't uttered a word since she said the names to me," Rina said. "Just another way to try and connect with her. Could be nothing, though. She's going to be discharged soon."

"Maybe that's for the better, Rina. I worry you're becoming obsessed with this patient. You have already done some pretty out of character things for her."

"Well, I worry about her. What will she do after she is... discharged? I mean, what happened to her mother? Why did Amy tell me these names? Why are you one of them? What else could the names on the list have in common?"

"All of them were at our wedding," Jonas said. "We invited a lot of people from Holy Saints."

Rina raised her head. "That's true, we did."

Jonas looked around the room for the waiter. "Listen, if you don't want to have dinner with me, that's okay. You can go. Go play detective. I won't get mad. I'm just worried about what you're doing. I do find it sweet, though, that you worry so much about your ex-husband. Are you trying to save me, Rina? Only you would ever want to save an ex-husband."

Rina laughed. "I guess I can stay. I do need to eat before work."

"I wish we were at home, having pizza with Denzel on the couch instead." Jonas put his hand up, trying to catch the waiter's attention.

Rina laughed. "I'm worried he's too scared to come back to our table.

CHAPTER 23

When they finished dinner at Giovanni's, Jonas insisted on coming to Rina's home, the one they used to share, to visit Denzel. Rina knew it was an obvious tactic to go back to their house, but agreed.

The date, if you could call it that, went well. Rina had forgotten how charming Jonas could be. She laughed willingly at his jokes, and genuinely enjoyed his company. It was almost how it used to be, before they separated. It was almost as if Rina felt the way she had before... everything changed.

Maybe Jonas was right; marriage counselling could work. They'd wed each other for a reason. After tonight, Rina knew that spark of what made them work together was still there.

Even though they departed from the restaurant's parking lot at the same time, Jonas was already waiting in the driveway for Rina when she arrived. Instead of parking in the garage, she parked beside him. It seemed only customary for the man to walk a woman to their doorstep anyway.

Rina stepped out of her car, and Jonas exited his. She locked eyes with him for a moment and could feel the rush of shyness.

Jonas reached his hand out. "I want you to know, I had a fun time tonight. I hope we can do it again sometime."

Rina smiled. "I would love that, thanks for... showing me what a good time is again. Denzel is a lousy date."

"I know it." Jonas laughed. He guided Rina to her home. "I won't stay long, I promise. I just want to see him for a few minutes."

"No problem," Rina said. She turned the key and opened the door. "It feels weird, inviting you inside this house."

"Feels amazing to me." He stepped inside and yelled for Denzel. The fluffy brown poodle wagged its tail furiously as it ran and jumped into Jonas's midsection. "Whoa, boy." He patted his head and scratched along the side of his long neck under his ears. Denzel tilted his head to the side, his tail waving even faster. "I miss you too," Jonas said.

Rina smiled again but couldn't hide the shame. They agreed when they separated that she would keep Denzel – after all, he was a gift to her – but seeing Jonas with him now made her sad.

"How about you take him to your place overnight?" Rina said. "Maybe a few days. I can come by later and grab him."

"Are you sure?" Jonas said. "I would love a visit."

"Of course I'm sure," Rina said. "After all, he is our fur baby, and you're his dad." She laughed. "Besides, it will give me a reason to check out where you've been living. I imagine pizza boxes and empty beer bottles everywhere with a sink full of dishes."

"You'd be surprised. I was the messy one when we lived together, but I'm not how I used to be. I think you rubbed off on me in a good way."

"That will be worth seeing for myself."

Jonas smiled. "People change, Rina. I know I have." Rina smiled back. "So," Jonas said, clapping his hands, "when you pick him up, we can do pizza and a movie at my place, then? I'll hide the rest of the pizza boxes before you come. We can call it date number two?"

She couldn't contain how happy his words were making her. "I guess so – that is if you consider tonight date number one."

"Well, I can't speak for you, but I do," Jonas's pet Denzel on the head and the dog licked the side of his face. "See, I even got a kiss at the door before leaving. It's definitely a date."

Rina laughed. "I'll see you soon."

Jonas grabbed a leash hanging beside the door and connected it to Denzel's collar. "Goodnight, Rina. I—" For a moment he lowered his head. "I don't want to say anything stupid to mess this up."

"I love you too," Rina said.

Jonas looked up at her, his eyes watering. "You don't know how long I wanted to hear that." He turned to leave, but Rina grabbed his shoulder. When Jonas turned, Rina kissed him softly.

"You don't know how long I wanted to do that again, too," Rina said with a smile. "You are right to be worried about me. Sometimes, I worry myself. I haven't taken care of myself, after what happened with... Jenny. It's weird, it took tonight, our time together, what Sarah told me, for me to see how much damage I've done."

"I just want you to be okay. No matter what. This may be something I shouldn't say, but I'm stupid. I hate to ruin anything about this moment, but... since we've been apart, I've never been with anyone else. Since you, there's been no one else I care for."

Rina smiled. "That's not messing up the moment. I wanted to know, even though I would never ask. I think you were right about a few things. Maybe we could do some counseling together. Sarah, she's been pushing me to take some time off. Maybe I should take it." Rina lowered her head. "I need to start thinking about myself again."

"Maybe..." He didn't finish and looked away.

"What is it?" Rina asked. "It's okay, you can say it."

"Maybe we can take that honeymoon we never had," Jonas finished. "I know – too soon. With the new hospital opening, I know it will be busy. I just want to spend quality time with you."

"When would you want to go? And where?" Rina asked with a smile.

"Anywhere that has a beach with fruity alcoholic drinks is all I want with you for a weekend. And as for when, whenever you can."

"I'd love to. I'll talk to Sarah in the morning."

"I can't believe this is happening right now. I never thought we could get back to a moment like this. I—" He smiled. "—can't believe it."

Rina nodded. "I know we have a lot to talk about, but maybe a vacation is a good way to start those conversations. I'll talk to Sarah and let you know."

"I'll shop around for trips, and let you know too." Jonas stepped closer and kissed Rina once more. "I love you, too," he whispered. "C'mon boy!" Denzel jumped up and headed to Jonas's car. Jonas opened the door and the dog jumped in. Jonas waved bye before getting inside.

Rina waved back, watching her ex-husband and her dog leave the driveway. She smiled until she shut the door. For a moment she panicked.

She hadn't been in her house alone for some time. Denzel was always there, giving her a comforting feeling. Rina breathed in deep. She talked to herself, telling herself she would be okay.

She sighed at the idea of a beach vacation with Jonas. Even the short kisses he gave her sent her head spinning. She'd forgot how well he kissed. Her mind jumped immediately to how the first night would go in their hotel room when they left. Would she willingly let things go further? Should they take their time?

Was she setting their rekindling of their marriage up for disaster already by agreeing to a trip with him? It felt right in the moment, but was she rushing back into their relationship?

Rina went into her bedroom. She had the sudden urge to go out for a run. Instead, for a change she put on comfy clothes and grabbed a bag of potato chips from the pantry and plopped herself onto the couch.

She turned on the television and ate a few chips. While searching for something to watch she remembered what Jonas had told her about the names on Amy Deaver's list.

She got off the couch and went into the basement, searching for the box. She smiled when she saw the one labeled

"Wedding." She opened it and started searching through the pictures.

Their wedding had been large. Jonas insisted on inviting many of the hospital staff, especially management. He said it was always a wise choice to make friends in high places if you could. She glanced through a stack of photos.

It didn't take long for her to find Jonas, his arm wrapped around Dr. Caleb Jansen. They had always been close. He was only a few years older than Jonas, but their friendship blossomed the moment the surgeon started working at Holy Saints. It was good to know that Jonas and he were still close with poker nights.

Rina spotted another picture with Phyllis Deaver in it. Even in the picture she seemed to be upset. She could only imagine why Phyllis had been angry at the moment it was taken. It could be she was upset the picture was being taken to begin with. Behind her, Jonas was laughing, talking to someone that Rina couldn't make out.

The next photo made Rina smile again. It was one of her and Jonas kissing during their first dance. A group of people huddled around watching them.

Rina noticed one of the people in the crowd was Ron Alder. His arm was wrapped around a woman wearing a black dress with an emerald green necklace. Rina squinted and nearly dropped the photo when she realized Marie Deaver was at her wedding. The face was the same on Phyllis's wall.

Rina shook her head. The woman who she had become obsessed about was at her wedding. She grabbed her phone, about to call Jonas. Had he known she was at the wedding too?

Phyllis had said they weren't together for too long. Jonas said he didn't really know Marie Deaver that well.

How could Rina have forgotten Marie was there that night? The wedding day was hectic, of course. The reception was busy as well. Rina thought she would have remembered Marie, though.

Rina grabbed the next photo, and it was all of them. Adam

Greber, Ron Alder, Phyllis Deaver, Jonas. All of them were sitting at a round table, raising their cups when the picture was taken. Marie Deaver was next to Jonas.

CHAPTER 24

When Rina arrived at work, she felt like a new woman. She was no longer the Dr. Rina Kent who left work that morning. She felt a hundred pounds lighter than the other Rina.

Even after seeing a picture of Marie Deaver at their wedding, she put everything back into the box, and left it in her basement. She wasn't going to keep pursuing whatever she was after.

She walked past the rec area and amongst the patients she easily spotted Amy sitting at her table with a puzzle. Rina wondered when she would be discharged. Perhaps there was no good answer for how to treat a young woman like Amy. She hoped that Belinda could help Phyllis when Amy was being discharged. If she left the ward with a safety plan, she would hope her colleague would be following up to ensure everything was working at home.

She caught her anxious thoughts and stopped herself. Amy was not her responsibility. Jonas was right; Rina felt the need to save people. That wasn't up to her, though. She could only help people where help was possible. For Amy, she hoped the young woman would be okay, but she was not her patient.

Rina had a primary goal at work today. To her delight, she spotted Sarah in her office. Now Rina wouldn't have to wait until the morning to ask.

Rina knocked on her door. "Hey," she said, opening it to come inside. "Are you busy?"

Sarah put up her hands with a smile. "When are we not?"

"Hopefully, this won't be too much to ask. I know things are busy, like you said, things are always busy, but I wanted to take you up on your offer."

"What do you mean?"

"For some time away. I wanted to take a last-minute vacation – with Jonas." Rina smiled. Sarah shared the same expression.

"Wow, I'm excited for you, Rina. I didn't know you two were talking."

"Yeah, it just sort of happened. I'm just as surprised."

Sarah nodded. "Well, wow! That's great. When were you hoping to leave?"

"Would this weekend be, okay? I know it's last minute."

"More like last second." Sarah laughed. "I'm happy for you, and I think you need some time away. Approved!" Rina almost jumped for joy but instead smiled again and thanked her profusely. "Where are you two going?" Sarah asked.

"Somewhere with a beach. And fruity drinks were Jonas's demand."

"Did Jonas get time away approved too?"

"I'm sure he's working his magic right now to get it off as well. Are you sure I'm not putting you out by taking this time? I don't want to hurt the ward or impact the patients in a negative way."

Sarah shook her head. "Not at all. I think this will be good for you. Have a drink on the beach for me." Rina thanked her again and went to leave but Sarah called out. "Sorry, wait." Rina turned back. "I'm sorry – for this morning. I feel like I was a little rough. Maybe I need time off too."

"Well, I'll have a fruity alcoholic drink for you," Rina said. "And I know that I've been... difficult lately. I hope to change that."

Sarah smiled. "I'm happy for you, Rina."

"Me too," Rina admitted. "I mean, I'm happy. Soon too, all of us will be in the new hospital."

Sarah let out a heavy sigh. "That's another matter that

has me stressed. They pulled in management for an emergency meeting. Turns out the hospital opening is going to be delayed... indefinitely, at the moment."

"Why?"

"Money." Sarah shook her head. "Isn't it always money. Apparently, there are funding issues that need to be worked out. It goes over my head completely, but they have a money issue."

"I guess we're all stuck at Holy Saints for a while more; perfect."

"I'm sure you heard about the funeral service for Adam?" Sarah said, changing the subject. "It's next weekend."

"I didn't know that. Maybe me, you and Belinda could go together."

"I'd like that."

Rina left Sarah's office and walked down the hall towards her own. As she passed Belinda's she heard her talking on the phone. She appeared to be whispering but doing a lousy job.

"That's not what I said," Belinda hissed to the person on the phone. "What did you—" When she spotted Rina, she smiled and waved, closing her door.

Rina stepped into her own office. On top of her desk was a white package. Her smile vanished when she saw it.

She opened the package, her mouth dropping when she saw the puzzle, a special puzzle that she'd ordered to work with Amy. Rina felt like throwing it away. She didn't want it anymore. All she wanted was to leave on a plane with Jonas and not look back.

She went down the hall to Belinda's office. She knocked once and waited for her to open. Instead, she heard Belinda still talking on the phone.

Rina looked at the box, then down the hall. She walked slowly to the rec room, peering at Amy playing with the puzzle that was on her table.

"Hey, Dr. Kent," Bethany said, standing beside her. She leaned into her shoulder. "I want you to know I didn't know Dr. Alloy would be so hard on you. I couldn't not report what I saw. I can't jeopardize my job... I need it. I hope you understand."

Rina nodded at her, still watching Amy. "I most certainly do. I haven't been myself lately, and I'm sorry too." Bethany smiled. "Hey," Rina asked, "do you have a marker I could borrow?"

"I'm sure I can find one in the nurse's room." Bethany grabbed one for her.

Rina opened the puzzle box and started writing on the pieces with the marker.

"What is that?" Bethany asked.

"Something I got for Amy," Rina answered. Bethany had a look of concern. "It's something good, don't worry."

Rina walked into the rec room and up to Amy, who didn't seem to care she was near her, and continued to hum her song.

"I got you something, Amy," Rina said. "Is it okay if I sit with you to show you?"

Amy didn't answer or give her any attention. Rina waited another moment before grabbing a chair and sitting on the other side of the table.

"I think you're going to love it," Rina said. "I got you a puzzle. A new puzzle. I'm sure you have done all the ones in the rec room a million times over." Amy stopped humming for a moment. "How about I take this puzzle and just move it to the side?" Rina swiped her hand across the table, moving the pieces, making sure not to ruin the ones that were connected.

She made enough space for the puzzle she'd made for Amy. She dropped the pieces in front of her. "Try this one," Rina said.

Amy started sorting the pieces quickly. There were only a few of them, and only three that had words on them; the rest were white.

Within a few minutes, Amy had put it together and smiled.

"Hello Amy, I'm Dr. Rina Kent," the finished puzzle read.

Rina reached into her pocket and dropped the marker in front of Amy. "You can write on them too if you want. Then I have to put it together."

Amy looked at the puzzle, and for a quick moment, at Rina. She grabbed the marker, and popped off the cap.

CHAPTER 25

Other patients and staff began to surround Rina and Amy as they continued to communicate with the puzzle. Rina had luckily purchased several boxes. Each box contained several blank puzzle piece collections that you could write on. Rina would write out a sentence and Amy would answer, then write her own.

Rina smiled when she noticed how much fun Amy was having. Her smile widened when she saw Sarah and Belinda join the crowd.

"Isn't it something," Bethany said to them.

Sarah shrugged. "That's just... Rina."

Belinda whispered something under her breath. When Rina looked up at her colleague, she thought she would find a welcoming face, like the rest; instead, Belinda seemed to be almost upset.

Rina took her time in writing out her next puzzle to Amy. "If you can, Amy," Rina said before giving it to her, "and this might be a tough question to answer, but let's see how you do."

Rina pushed the puzzle in front of Amy. Amy completed it in a few minutes. This time however, she didn't seem eager to answer.

"Why are you here?" the puzzle read.

"Do you need some privacy?" Rina said. She looked at the audience and asked them to leave.

"Let's go, everyone," Bethany said, assisting with crowd control.

Rina watched Amy look at the puzzle. "Take some time with this one," she said. She held up a finger. "One moment. I will be right back." She stood and smiled at Sarah.

"Let's have a quick chat in the conference room," Sarah said. Belinda followed them. When the three of them were inside, they exchanged shocked expressions.

"I didn't think it would work, but it did," Rina said, laughing. "We have mostly been making small talk. Amy's sentence structure is limited. We knew that would be the case, but she can explain things."

"That's incredible," Sarah said, patting her on the shoulder. "How did you even think of this?"

Rina shrugged. "I thought there could be a way to communicate through puzzles, since she's obsessed with them. There's a product to purchase for most things these days."

"It's too bad you didn't share your idea before," Belinda said coldly. "Tomorrow afternoon she's being discharged."

Rina looked at Sarah. "Is that right?"

"Belinda already wrote up the safety plan for Phyllis. She's coming tomorrow after her clinical time ends at the pediatrician clinic. She will likely take Amy home then."

"I need more time with her," Rina said. "There's so much we don't know. Amy could start to open up more."

"You just asked me for time off for a vacation. What are you doing?"

"I know, but this is a breakthrough. I need to see this one through, Sarah. She's going to be discharged before I leave anyway."

"Let's try it." Sarah looked at Belinda. "You've done great work with Amy, but I'm thinking given the progress made today that Rina should take over the case from here and be her assigned psychiatrist. There could be more we can discover with this young lady."

Belinda nodded reluctantly. "Of course. Our main objective is to take care of Amy."

"Great work, Rina. Feels good to say that to you." Sarah

smiled before leaving the room.

Belinda agreed. "She's right, good work. I wish I had thought of it." She turned to leave but Rina reached out for her.

"Is everything okay?" Rina asked.

"Fine. It's... been busy lately. I'm going to go home. Have a good night shift."

"You have a good night too. By the way, I was hoping, maybe when I come back from my vacation, we could talk about the night shift again. I've been doing them a lot, at my request, but I'm thinking if it would be best for me to go back to a rotation again. Would that be okay?"

Belinda smiled, but her eyes stayed expressionless. "Sure. Let's talk when you get back."

Rina left the conference room with Belinda, and Amy was already standing from the table. Cody Alder had taken the puzzle pieces and put them back in the box.

"What are you doing?" she asked.

"It's night routine, Dr. Kent," he said with a smirk. He waved over Bethany. "I think Amy's ready for bed; can you bring her, please."

Bethany beamed at Amy. "Okay, sweetheart, it's that time again. I know you like your new puzzle, but we can play with it some more with Dr. Kent in the morning."

"Good night, Amy," Rina said. "I'll see you bright and early."

Amy followed the nurse towards the bedrooms.

"How did your little talk with my father go last night?" Cody asked.

"You were there last night?" Rina said, confused.

"I saw you when I drove to my father's house," he said. "Funny, he wouldn't answer the door for me, but then I see you coming down the street."

"You were watching me last night?" Rina asked.

"You." Cody's tone turned nasty. "Always trying to *get me* on something. Can't you just... leave me alone. Dad didn't show up to work today. I guess you'll have to see him tomorrow. Talk about me then."

"This has nothing to do with you."

"Right," he said with a smile. "I'm done playing games for him, and with you." Cody abruptly started walking down the hall, before turning with a wide smile. "You and he don't have to worry though; I won't *say a word*." His smile grew when he saw the shock on Rina's face.

CHAPTER 26

Rina attempted to call Jonas, but it went straight to his voicemail. Does Cody know about Amy's list. How could he know? Had Amy whispered the names to him? Now Ron Alder unexpectedly didn't show up to work.

Rina had promised not to make things worse, but she needed to make sure Ron was home. If he was, she could relax her mind and not jump to the worst conclusions. What if he wasn't home? What if something terrible had happened? What if she was right about Amy's list?

Part of her wanted to call the police, but she wasn't sure what she would say, or how crazy she would come off.

A man didn't show up to work today! Send the police!

Rina made another excuse to leave the ward. It was a little past nine at night. She wasn't going to leave his home until Ron Alder opened the door.

As she drove to 1545 Rosewind Street, she tried to call Jonas several times. She needed him to calm her, tell her to stop acting crazy. Him not picking up made it worse. She drove faster and got to her destination much quicker than the day before.

She got out of the car, taking a moment to look out into the woods where she'd thought she saw someone hiding the night prior. The sun was setting now, giving her the comfort of daylight. When it was dark yesterday, the woods had a much more ominous presence.

When did Cody see her coming to his father's home? Was it Cody she saw inside?

Rina walked up the steps and knocked hard on the front door. Like yesterday, nobody answered. She backed up to look into the windows. She saw no movement or lights on. She rang the doorbell and knocked again. She waited patiently, but still nothing.

Just as she had the night before, she went around the side gate. Like yesterday, the same light was on in an upstairs bedroom.

"I'm not leaving this time," Rina said. "He's opening that door."

Rina went back to the front door and knocked harder. "I know you're home!" she yelled. "Please, this is important!" Luckily for her, there were only a few neighbors living on the same block. All of the homes had expensive cars in the driveway. Ron's black Escalade was still parked in his.

Rina knocked again, harder, and the door slipped open. Rina took a step back. "Hello! Ron! It's Rina – Dr. Rina Kent. We need to talk." When she heard no one, she pushed the door open more. She knew better than to step inside. She didn't want to break into the man's home. The last thing she wanted was to give him a reason to go after her more.

Rina was certain he was home though. His vehicle was parked in the same spot. The light from the day before was on. She hadn't seen anybody inside like yesterday, but she was certain someone was home.

The door slowly opened fully. She called his name again. Rina looked inside the living room. Dark leather furniture faced a large brick fireplace. A metal poker sat in its clasp on the side of it. Embers still glittered red inside the ash pile inside the pit.

The sound of a phone ringing from the other side of the living room made her jump. From the front entrance, she spotted a cell phone on a nightstand beside an empty chair.

"Hello?" Rina called out. She looked back towards the living room. The circular couch had a blanket hanging over one side. When Rina took her time to look again, she saw the blanket was covering something larger.

She looked at the wood floor beneath her. Footprints were imprinted in a dark substance that led to the front door. Rina breathed in deep and turned to leave. She nearly screamed when her hand touched a brownish dried liquid on the doorknob.

She looked back at the blanket on the couch. "Mr. Alder!" she called out. She went around the couch to see. The small blanket covered the torso of a body. Extending out the sides were hands, and partially covered bare feet.

Rina removed the blanket slowly. The cold, dead eyes of Ron Alder looked back at her. His mouth was permanently grimacing. A deep cut ran across his entire neckline.

CHAPTER 27

"None of this makes any sense!" Detective Hicks yelled. He leaned on Rina's car as he took notes.

Rina continued to shake as she told the detective how she found Ron Alder in his living room. She watched as officers entered the home with duffle bags. A large van marked "Crime Scene Investigation" parked nearby.

"This is the second murder I'm involved with you on," Hicks said. "I need you to tell me what is really going on here! Why did you come to Ron Alder's house today?"

"I was worried for my husband, my ex-husband." Rina said, struggling with her words. "Please, send someone to his home right away."

"Why?" Hicks said. "What does the murder of Mr. Alder have to do with your ex-husband?"

"He's in danger!" Rina yelled. "I'll tell you everything, please. Just tell me someone is on their way to his home."

Detective Hicks made a click with his mouth. He asked Rina for Jonas's address and made a request on his radio to send a squad car to do a check.

"Now, start talking!" Hicks said, folding his arms.

A car drove up the street and parked beside the police vehicles. Sarah got out and ran towards Rina. "I got your text! Is everything okay?"

"He's dead. Ron Alder was murdered."

Sarah shook her head in disbelief. She looked at Detective Hicks and he nodded.

"Now," he said with a sound of irritation. "Why are you here, Mrs. Kent?"

"Amy Deaver," Rina blurted out.

Sarah looked at her, confused. "What?"

"Who's that?" Hicks asked, slightly annoyed.

"She's a patient at the psych ward at Holy Saints," Sarah answered. "What's happening, Rina?"

"I lied to you," Rina said, turning to her. "That night when Amy got out of her room, she came into the gym. I told you nothing happened, but I lied. She whispered a bunch of names to me. Her journal! Last night I looked inside it. She had the same names listed in it as well."

"What?" Sarah asked. "Why did you lie?"

"I don't know," Rina said, shaking her head. "The first name she said was Adam Greber. Then I find out he's dead, murdered. The next was Ron Alder. Now he's been killed too."

"Who else is on this list of names?" Hicks said, raising his voice.

"Phyllis Deaver and Jonas, my ex-husband."

Hicks looked at Sarah. "Dr. Alloy, do you know where Phyllis Deaver lives?"

Sarah nodded, but it was Rina who answered with an address. "The second house on that road, along the private beach area. It's a white house."

Hicks looked at Rina sternly a moment before calling for another patrol car.

Rina looked at Sarah. "I told Jonas about the list yesterday. I thought maybe it was just a coincidence that Adam Greber was killed, and he was one of the names on Amy's list. Then, Cody said his father didn't show up to work today. I was worried, and had to see for myself."

Hicks looked at Sarah again. "Is he at Holy Saints right now, Cody, the son? I'll need to talk to him right away too."

"His shift ended. I'll have to look his address up at the office," Sarah said.

Detective Hicks pointed at Rina. "You," he said. "You need

to show the crime scene crew everything that you touched. Everywhere that you walked. Anywhere where you were inside this house, they need to know."

"Is Jonas okay?" Rina asked, ignoring him. "The car you sent to check, did they get to his home yet?"

Hicks held up his hand. "There's a lot that we have to sort out here. I'll radio for an update. First, I need you to come with me. You," he said looking at Sarah. "Go back to Holy Saints; I'll have one of my guys follow. I need you to get me the address of the son. Then I need to talk to your patient, Amy. I'll need to speak with her right away. She has a list of names. We need to find out why."

"That's what I've been trying to figure out since she told me their names," Rina said, taking a deep breath.

"Okay, Rina, I'll bite. What did you find out?"

"I think everyone on the list has something to do with Amy's mother."

Hicks nodded. "Right. Do we have her address? The patient is over eighteen, I hope. If so, I don't need the mom's permission, but let's connect with the mom too. Have that address ready right away. Let my guy know and he will call her," he said to Sarah.

Sarah's jaw dropped. "That's going to be hard," she said. "Marie Deaver's missing."

"Jesus, I need some more coffee tonight." Hicks turned to Rina. "Deaver," he repeated. "That was a name on the list too, right?"

"Phyllis Deaver," Rina repeated. "It's her aunt. Amy's been living with her for some time and stayed with her after her mother left."

"Left? Where did she go? Is she missing or did she leave?"

"Phyllis tells me the cops that were looking into her disappearance closed the case," Rina said. "They believe she's somewhere in the Vancouver area."

Hicks raised his eyebrows. "Did you discover anything else, Rina? Now is the time to tell me everything."

"I... don't know. Marie Deaver was a patient at Holy Saints with Adam Greber. Ron Alder dated Marie before she went missing. Phyllis said they had an explosive fight before they ended things. Phyllis is Marie's sister. Jonas—"

"What about Jonas?" Hicks asked. He looked at Sarah, whose jaw was still hanging open listening to everything. "You can leave now, Dr. Alloy." Hicks whistled at a cop walking by and told him to follow Sarah back to the hospital, with instructions.

"Collect everything I asked of you and tell my officer," Hicks said to Sarah.

Sarah got back into her car. The cop ran towards his cruiser to follow her.

"What about your ex-husband?" Hicks repeated to Rina. "Why would he be on the list?"

"Jonas – he provided care to Amy when she got to the hospital. Amy, she tried to kill herself. Jonas pumped her stomach and saved her. I don't know why he would be on the list, though."

"I'll get Amy Deaver to answer that," Hicks said confidently.

Rina smiled and chuckled.

"Now what?"

"She has autism. She's mostly a non-verbal autistic. The only words she said to me were the names."

Hicks took in a deep breath. "I'm going to have one hell of a night here."

"She's starting to talk to me now, only through a puzzle that you write on. She likes puzzles. I bought one where she can write on the pieces to communicate. She's really taken to it."

"Good. When we get back to the hospital, you are going to help your patient talk to me. We need to figure out why these people are on a list of names your patient has, and why they are being killed."

"That's the frustrating part of this. I know Amy won't say."

"We will make her!" Hicks barked. "We can talk to her

through the puzzle, you said." When he saw no response from Rina he nodded. "Okay, why won't Amy talk about it?"

Rina shook her head. "It's what I've been trying to figure out. It all has to do with her mother. What her mother told her in Amy's journal. The list of names Amy whispered. What I saw written in her other journal. All of it is instructions to Amy." Hicks looked at her, not understanding. "Somehow, even Cody Alder knows it. *Don't say a word.*"

CHAPTER 28

Rina looked at Amy across the conference room table. The puzzle pieces were in front of her, with a marker beside her hand. Amy hadn't picked it up once to write on the puzzle pieces since Sarah Alloy and the officer escorted her to the room.

Amy rocked in her chair, looking around at all the faces in the room quickly. Detective Hicks stood behind Rina, instructing Rina to write certain questions on the puzzle, but Amy ignored them all.

"Why did you say the names?" one puzzle read. "Why Jonas Kent?" "Why Phyllis Deaver?" "Why Adam Greber?" "The police can help." "Please tell us."

Several other cops in the room had their notepads open, waiting for a response from the girl. Sarah leaned against the wall.

Rina looked around at them. "Maybe it should just be me and her," she said. "Too many people."

"I'm staying," Hicks barked. "I need to hear everything you say to her and potentially anything she says back."

"She's not going to say anything or write anything with you in the room, that's for sure. I'm her psychiatrist. I'm the only one she spoke to."

"Your ex-husband is also on the list," Hicks said. "I can't leave you with a witness like that, especially since you weren't exactly forthcoming before."

"Leave the door open," Rina said. "Put your ear to the door. Place a camera in the room. Do whatever you need to feel comfortable."

Detective Hicks nearly turned red. "I can't—" An officer from outside the room whispered something to him. He nodded. "Rina, can we chat outside for a moment?"

Rina stood up and told Amy she would be right back. She followed Hicks out of the conference room. A small group watched them. Rina spotted Belinda and Bethany talking to officers separately. Sarah followed her out, talking on the phone, her other hand wiping her forehead. Several police officers stood guard.

Hicks went down the hallway, stopping near the rec room. Rina spotted an officer talking to Ryan, the security guard, before the detective turned to her with a sympathetic look for a change.

"He wasn't home," Detective Hicks said. "Jonas. The officers said the apartment was empty except for a brown poodle."

"Denzel," Rina said, her heart beating fast. "The cops, they found nothing at his home?"

"Now, I need your help, Rina. We're looking for him, but I need you to figure out what this young woman knows, okay?"

"Okay," Rina answered. They returned to the conference room. Rina nodded at Hicks and closed the door partly, him waiting outside.

Rina looked across the table at Amy and grabbed the puzzle box, moving it across the table. "Jonas is missing," Rina whispered. "I know you might not know how to tell me, but I need your help."

Rina grabbed a marker and started writing on the puzzle. She put the broken pieces in front of her and waited.

Amy looked at Rina for a quick moment, and back at the puzzle.

"Where is mom?" the puzzle read.

Amy lowered her head. She began rocking back and forth. After a moment she started to hum the song.

Rina smiled, a tear forming in her eye. "Please, Amy. Try

and tell me." Rina picked up the marker and put it in Amy's hand. Rina knew there was a high chance Amy wasn't capable of answering her question. Her mother had also told her to not say a word.

Rina looked at Amy as she hummed her song. "None of this is your fault," she whispered to the girl. "None of it."

Amy continued to hum the song, and Rina started to sing. "Ladybird, Ladybird, fly away home. Your house is on fire and your children are gone." She lowered her head in defeat.

The door swung open, and Phyllis Deaver stormed in, her eyes wide and full of rage. "What are you doing?" Detective Hicks and Sarah walked into the room behind her. Phyllis turned to Detective Hicks. "Why are you interviewing my mute niece? What the hell kind of treatment do you provide here?" she barked at Sarah. "What the hell is going on?"

Detective Hicks spoke up. "I think you and I need to talk."

"I know about the murders, and the list of names," she said back. "Your officer already spoke with me. I told him everything I had to share."

"I need you to talk to me now."

"I need to talk to your *boss!*" Phyllis yelled. "Did I give any of you permission to speak to my niece about a murder? You understand she has a disability, right? Look at her, she's scared." She pointed at Amy, who continued to rock in the chair. "What you have done tonight is completely wrong! I should have been here before you talked to my niece! You talked to her about murder! She's got no clue what's going on."

"We didn't say anything about murder," Rina said. "We were trying to find out why the names were on the list."

"This *list!*" Phyllis yelled. "Now we hear about the list! Why didn't you say something earlier? Were you waiting for me to get killed before you did something? You were snooping around my house that day when I was supposed to be at the hospital. Jonas is on the list too, Rina! I feel like this crap detective needs to be asking you more questions too."

"Please stay, Mrs. Deaver," Detective Hicks asked. "We're

trying to get to the bottom of this."

"It's past one in the morning! You scared my niece to death. I'm taking her home."

"She hasn't been discharged," Rina said.

Sarah stepped in. "I spoke with Phyllis about this. Given everything that's happened here—" She looked at Rina and back at Phyllis. "—we will discharge her with a safety plan like we discussed."

"Give me the paperwork later," Phyllis said. "I'm taking her home now. She needs good sleep for a change." She looked at the puzzle. "And what is that?"

"She's started to communicate with us using a puzzle."

"She's talking to you? I wasn't informed of any of this. I asked for updates," she barked at Sarah. "All I get is lies from her psychiatrist, and detectives harassing my disabled niece." She went around the table and grabbed Amy's hand, forcing her off the chair. "We are leaving, Amy. We are going home. Let's go."

"Mrs. Deaver!" Hicks called to her.

Phyllis waved him off. "Enough! Enough. That's enough for one night. I'm not coming into work tomorrow," she yelled at Sarah. "I'm going to take some time with my niece and take some time with my lawyers. You will hear from them soon, believe me. The care this facility has provided my niece is a joke." She looked at Hicks. "Come in the morning if you need more from me. I'm done with this tonight."

Detective Hicks pursed his lips. "Very well. In the morning. I'll have a patrol come by once in a while to check on your safety tonight."

Phyllis nodded. "Good. Now get out of my way." The detective listened and Phyllis dragged Amy behind her. Phyllis looked back at Rina. "I used to think so highly of you." She left, giving Sarah a cold stare before exiting the room.

Another officer entered the conference room and whispered to Detective Hicks. Hicks shook his head profusely, looking at Rina.

Rina turned and saw Sarah walking towards her, taking

in a deep breath. She sat across the table from her.

"What a mess," she said. "What a mess."

"I know," Rina said. "I should have said something right away when Amy told me those names. What about Amy?"

"Belinda is going to take her back and do some outpatient work with her. I don't want you anywhere near the patient now."

Rina lowered her head. "I… understand."

"I don't think you do. I— You need to take some extended time off, Rina. The hospital is going to run their own investigation. You heard Phyllis. She will look to litigate. This isn't what we need right now with the new hospital delays… We can't afford a legal battle over this. You need to participate in whatever the hospital investigation wants from you. I don't know if I can help you keep your job this time, Rina." Sarah stood up. "I can't pay you while you're off either. This is considered leave with no pay. I've been instructed to tell you to speak with your union official if you have any concerns on that."

Rina kept her head down, not wanting to look at Sarah's face. She knew the disappointment it would show. "I… understand."

Sarah let out a heavy breath. "Just when I thought you were getting better, Rina. For a moment I thought the old you was here. The psychiatrist that I… was jealous of. The psychiatrist I strived to be. What the hell happened?"

Rina looked up at her. "I wish— I know what it is. The day Jenny Berange killed herself. I should have listened to you. To Jonas. To everyone. I should have gotten help. Now I'm in this situation. Jonas… is missing."

"He's not home?" Sarah asked with concern.

"Detective Hicks just told me,"

Sarah went around the table and patted her on the shoulder. "I'm going to go home for the night. Whatever you do, Rina, make sure you take care of yourself this time." She patted her on the shoulder again before leaving. "Maybe you should grab some things from your office, if you need them."

Rina watched Sarah walk out. She took in several breaths,

wondering how she'd managed to mess up everything in her life. She slowly made her way down the hall to her office. Once inside, she shut the door, and sat at her desk, covering her face with her fingers. She fought back the tears as she grabbed her backpack and shoved a few personal items into it. Rina's despair disappeared momentarily when she saw the puzzle box. It was the one Amy had worked on before Cody put it away.

"It was a good idea," Rina said to herself, "and it worked." She'd managed to have a breakthrough with a difficult patient. She felt pride in that accomplishment. She put the puzzle box in her bag.

Her office door swung open, and Detective Hicks looked sternly at her. "The security guard on the ward, Ryan, said you left at the beginning of your shift yesterday to grab ''some files' from your home. He said when he saw you return you didn't have anything on you. Where did you go?"

Rina slowly nodded. "Ron Alder's house."

Detective Hicks shook his head. "Stand up." When Rina didn't immediately do so he repeated himself louder. "You need to come with me to the station this time."

CHAPTER 29

"Again, I must remind you of your right to a lawyer," Hicks said. "Also… If you're not going to tell me anything, why are we still talking?"

Rina shook her head. "I didn't do anything."

"Nothing at all," Hicks snickered back. "You lied to your own staff about what Amy Deaver said. You went to Ron Alder's house the night he was murdered, and didn't say anything." Rina looked up at him. "That's right! Forensics puts his time of death around the time you just so happened to visit him."

"I told you—"

"The person you saw through the window, right." Hicks shuffled in the interview room chair, which was too small for his body. Everything in the room was tinier than it should be. The table where Rina sat was almost fully consumed by Hicks's elbows as he yelled at her. It was if the room was designed to make you feel as though a man like Hicks was jumping down your throat.

"Cody Alder, he told me. 'Don't say a word'. He knows more, I know it."

Hicks shook his head. "And he's missing too. Cody Alder is missing. Your ex-husband is missing. You visited Ronald Alder the night he was killed."

"I didn't kill them," Rina shouted.

"Kill them?" Hicks repeated. "Are Jonas and Cody missing, or are they shot or cut up? Where's the gun, Rina? If you help me, I can help you. This can go down a few ways. Tell me what these people did to you. Tell me why you did it."

"Stop!" Rina shouted.

"It was no secret you hated Adam Greber. And Jonas, who wouldn't hate their ex? Ron Alder, you have issues with his son, and daddy threatened your job over it. And Phyllis Deaver? I can assume why Deaver would be on your list after getting to know her this morning."

"It's not my list," Rina said.

"Right, it's a mute autistic girl's list. The same girl who nobody ever heard talk besides you."

Rina rolled her eyes. "I have no reason to lie. The names are in her journal," Rina said. "Are your people still looking for Jonas? If you're just going to try and put me under a magnifying glass, I'll leave and look for him myself."

"We're still looking for him." Hicks nodded. "Him and Cody Alder. Now, what are you not telling me? You told the security guard you were going home. You already admitted you didn't. You visited Ron Alder. You see someone inside his home, you assume it was him and that he didn't want to open the door. Then you coincidentally go back the next day to see him again? Or was it to cover a crime?"

Rina scoffed. "Stop. Please. If I have to get a lawyer, I will. I need you to listen to me. Whoever did this to Ron and Adam is going to do it again to the other two on the list! You have her journal from the ward. I gave you the one I took from Phyllis's home."

"I also see that you tend to sneak off the ward, sometimes with excuses. You claimed you were working at the time of Adam Greber's death, but how do we know? Rina, I'll make things worse for you if you don't start telling me. Where's the gun? The knife?"

"I don't own a gun," Rina said.

Hicks sat back in his chair. "I feel like I'm playing catch-up with you every time I see you on a new development in the murder cases I'm involved with. If you don't start telling me what happened, we're going to make assumptions. I have cause to arrest you. I could keep you here for as long as I need until I get answers from you."

Rina stood up. "Well, I'm not under arrest. Right? I've played along with this for too long. I'm leaving."

Hicks stood up to respond when an officer knocked on the interview room door. Hicks opened it and they spoke in low voices.

Rina glanced up at the clock. It was already past two in the morning. Rina took out her phone and looked at it, hoping to see a new text from Jonas, but there was nothing.

Hicks shut the door and looked at her. "You can leave," he said. "I'll have one of my guys drop you off at your home. Thank you for speaking with me tonight. If I get an update on Jonas, I'll let you know, right away."

Rina was taken aback by the change in the detective's demeanor. "Okay," she agreed.

CHAPTER 30

Detective Hicks

Detective Hicks watched as Rina Kent got into a squad car. His patrolman waved to him before getting inside. Hicks nodded to him.

Another officer came up. "Sir, where do we go from here?"

"Good question, kid," Hicks said. He reached into his long jacket, trying to grab a smoke, and furrowed his brow when he forgot he quit yesterday. He had quit smoking many times over. Then a case like this would intertwine itself with him, and he would be craving the sweet taste of tobacco in his mouth. He claimed it helped him think, at least that's what he had told his wife.

Ex-wife, he reminded himself.

Seems like he had that in common with Dr. Kent. He wished he could reunite with Aileen Hicks. It had only been six months since they separated. There could still be a chance for it to mend. Was their marriage truly broken?

Hicks sneered at the idea of speaking to a psychiatrist like Rina to help fix his marriage. The woman was more of a mess than he was.

Aileen just got tired. Tired of Cormac Hicks's obsessiveness for solving every case he was assigned to, no matter what it took from her time with him. He understood why she left him. He was more surprised it hadn't happened ten years ago.

Still did not change the fact that it hurt more than anything Hicks had ever experienced on the job.

"Do you have a cig?" he asked the patrol officer. The man waved no. "Good for you. It's a bad habit."

After his men interviewed Ryan the guard, and learned the revelation of Rina visiting Ron Alder the night he was murdered, at the approximate time of death even, he'd thought he had solved what happened.

Rina did it.

She made up what Amy Deaver whispered to her. There was no solid alibi for her the day Greber was killed. That wouldn't explain the journals, though, he knew. How could Rina fabricate a journal with the list of names of people she wanted to kill?

His working theory had been blown to bits when the patrolman knocked on the interview room door. Another revelation had brought the investigation in an entirely new direction.

Searching the hospital, they found the knife that was used to kill Ron Alder. The knife was in a locker at Holy Saints being used by Cody.

The son killed the father. Hicks shook his head. Even after all this time on the job, and the ugliness he'd seen, he couldn't understand how a man could kill his own family. Hicks's own son would get so heated when he lived with him and Aileen. When his son was eighteen, he moved out and began adulthood right away, enlisting in the army. After he survived his tours, he came home, married and now had a young daughter.

Not that Hicks knew much about his granddaughter either.

All Hicks had was a job that sucked the life from him.

Where do we go from here? Hicks thought. It was a good question.

Detective Hicks looked at his patrolman. "Have men check the nearby bus stops, airports, and train stations. Have someone call the credit card companies. What we do is scour the streets of Carrington. We need to figure out where Cody Alder is before he kills again." Hicks started to walk towards his unmarked police car.

"Where are you going, sir?" the patrolman asked.

"Getting a pack of cigarettes," Hicks said. "Then going to Jonas Kent's home."

At the convenience store, he purchased a pack and a bag of chips, he ripped into the cigarette carton and pulled one out. He lit it and felt an overwhelming sense of calmness roll over him.

He looked at his watch. He hadn't slept in over twenty-four hours. He hadn't been home in nearly a whole day. No wonder his ex-wife hated him. The job was all he had left now. As much as he hated what he saw terrible people do, they gave him purpose. They let him feel alive, when he cuffed them and read them their rights.

There was nothing more satisfying than slapping a pair of cuffs on a person you knew committed a terrible crime.

Hicks parked his car beside Jonas Kent's apartment unit. He'd had one of his men call the apartment management ahead of time. The landlord was outside waiting for him.

"Mr. Kent lives on the fourth floor," the apartment manager said. "I knocked on his door already today, because of the dog. It's been barking for hours."

"Show me the way," Hicks said, pointing towards the door.

"Can you do something about the dog?"

Hicks laughed. "Call animal control when I leave." He almost felt annoyed at himself for not thinking ahead of time and having animal control at the apartment building as well. What if the dog was dangerous? Attacked him or the apartment manager? A lawsuit against the city wouldn't be what his boss would want.

"One moment," Hicks said, running back to his car. He grabbed the nearly empty bag of chips and came back to the front door. "Something for the mutt."

The office manager climbed the stairs with Hicks slowly following. He was tired, and almost felt sick with the lack of sleep.

At sixty-one, how much longer would he keep a schedule like this? The sleepless nights, the lurking thoughts of dead people taking over his mind day and night. It was too much, he knew. But... he also loved what he did.

The manager stood in front of the door. "Please stand back a moment," Hicks said. He pounded on the door. A dog began barking loudly, scratching at it. Hicks could hear no other movement besides the pet. "Police!" he yelled, banging on the door. The dog barked louder. "I'll take the key now," he said to the manager. He placed one hand on top of his holstered gun, and then opened the door a little. The snout of the dog poked out from the opening. Hicks grabbed the bag of chips from his pocket and threw them behind the dog.

The brown poodle wagged its tail and ate the crumbs off the floor. Hicks opened the door more. "Stay out here," he told the manager. He took out his weapon and closed the door. As he went past the dog, he patted it on his head.

"Where's your dad?" he asked. The dog jumped up at the side of the detective. Hicks patted it again before swiping him off. "Police!" he yelled. He searched the home, but Jonas Kent was certainly not there. He checked for anything that could give a clue as to where he was, having to pet the dog numerous times so it would let him search properly.

Nothing. Nothing except the dog. The medium-sized ball of brown fluff looked up at him, panting.

"Rina told me your name, boy... Denzel, right?" Hicks said. "Now what should I do with you?"

CHAPTER 31

Rina hadn't been home very long when a knock at her front door startled her. She opened it to see the grimacing face of Detective Hicks. At his side was Denzel, who barked at the sight of her.

"I checked Jonas's place. He's still missing but I found this guy." Detective Hicks let go of the leash. Denzel ran to Rina and jumped at her midsection. Rina lowered her head, and he licked her face profusely. "I figured you'd want him back."

"Thanks. Any leads on where Jonas could be?"

Detective Hicks shook his head. "I'm sorry, Mrs. Kent, but no. My men are putting in the hours tonight to find Jonas and arrest the one responsible for these murders."

Rina breathed heavily. "Call me Rina, Detective Hicks. You already accused me of murder; we may as well be less formal now. Are you here to question me more about these murders? Thank you for bringing Denzel back, but I can't handle your questions right now."

Detective Hicks nodded. "I don't mean to be rude. It's an old tactic. Wind someone up and see how they react. They get upset. They mess up their story and can't keep their lies straight. They tell me things they didn't mean to say when they're worked up. It's part of my job... I believe you now. Do you have any idea where Cody Alder could be?"

"You still haven't questioned him yet?" Rina asked, surprised.

"We can't find him or Jonas."

"I don't know where either of them is," Rina said. "I wish I did."

"If you see Cody, call 911 immediately," Hicks said. "We've found a strong connection between him and these murders."

Rina covered her mouth in shock. "What about Amy?" Rina asked. "Cody would talk to her at the ward. Whisper things to her. Phyllis Deaver said he would flirt with her too. Now Amy has told me a list of names Cody is murdering. Is she in danger?"

"I have one of my men patrolling around Phyllis Deaver's home tonight."

Rina wasn't happy with the answer. Then she remembered how easily she'd caught Rina trying to get into her home during the day. She had lights attached to her fence. The cameras inside. It wouldn't be easy to break into Phyllis Deaver's home, and even if they did, they would have to deal with her.

"I can put a patrol outside your home as well," the detective said.

Rina shook her head. "I'll be okay. I just want everyone you have looking for Jonas. Is there anything I can do?"

"Sleep. Leave it to us, Rina. If you can think of anything that could help with this investigation let me know immediately, otherwise, be patient, and get some sleep." He looked at his watch. "I need more coffee, I think."

Detective Hicks soon left. After giving Denzel water and food, she sat with the poodle, petting him. She remembered what Jonas said on their date. He wished he was at their home, eating pizza on the couch with her and Denzel.

An image of Ron Alder, covered in blood and his neck sliced open, intruded into Rina's thoughts. What would happen if they found Jonas that way? How could Rina continue living knowing her husband had been brutally murdered, and Rina could have helped him? Rina hit the side of the couch. If she hadn't lied about the list of names Amy told her, would Jonas have been okay? Would he be at their home, on the couch, having pizza?

Instead, he was... God knows where. Rina thought about

his parents. She was going to have to call them and tell them their son was missing. How long should she wait?

Be patient, Hicks had told her. Sleep, the detective said. How could she do either of those?

She grabbed Denzel's leash and connected it to his collar. "Time for a run," she said to him, and he waved his tail in response.

She grabbed her bag and tossed it on her shoulder. She didn't even bother changing her clothes. She needed to run. She needed to clear her mind.

She ran out the door, nearly forgetting to lock it. After several blocks her breath was more labored. It was unusual for her to be this tired already. She had to remind herself she barely slept the last few days.

She typically didn't run this late at night. With Jonas missing and the police searching for his son, the streets were more ominous than she remembered during the day. Shadows of bushes played tricks on her, thinking they were people. When she ran past buildings, she would stare down the empty alleys.

Where are you, Jonas? Rina thought. She ran faster, trying to tire her brain so it would stop showing her images of Jonas dead.

She stopped, and tried to regain her breath. She her bag from her shoulders and reached in to grab a bottle of water, frustrated when she realized she hadn't packed one. She didn't bring her cell. She hadn't prepared for this run at all.

She shook her head when she saw that all she had in her backpack was the puzzle Amy had written on, and other items she'd brought from the office. There was a twenty-four-seven convenience store down the block. She lightly jogged until she made it to the front door. When she opened it, a chime went off and the clerk stepped out from the back office.

"Hello," Rina said with a smile. "Just grabbing a drink." The man nodded and she went to the coolers at the side of the store. She grabbed a bottle of water and brought it to the counter. She made a face when she realized she didn't have her purse or money on her. "I'm so sorry," she said. "I didn't bring any money. Sorry to bother you." The man wished her a good night and Rina went back outside.

She sat under the lights of the convenience store on the curb, trying to catch her breath. She dug into her backpack, hoping she would find change or a loose bill at the bottom, but there was only the puzzle and her house keys.

Rina took out the box and shook it. She opened it and let some of the pieces from the box drop out. Rina smiled when she saw Amy had written on them.

Sarah said Belinda would be taking over her outpatient care now. She hoped Belinda would continue to use the puzzles to talk to her. There could be a lot to learn from Amy, not only about the investigation, but how to help her.

Rina assorted the puzzle from the pieces Amy had written on. Her smile vanished when she read the words.

She had asked Amy why she came to Holy Saints hospital.

Rina took in a deep breath as she read the puzzle again, wondering what Amy meant when she wrote the answer. "Aunt Phyllis," the puzzle read.

CHAPTER 32

Detective Hicks

Detective Hicks rolled down the window of his patrol car, grabbing another cigarette from the pack. It was his fifth one tonight already. Hell of a job he was doing quitting them, he thought. Hicks hated how such a small, rolled bunch of tobacco could have control over him.

It was a colder, windier night than usual. A gust knocked the cigarette out of his mouth as if it was on purpose. Hicks grabbed it and tossed it out the window, rolling it up.

The search for Cody Alder and Jonas Kent had brought nothing. Hicks knew in his gut more people would be killed or found dead before the sun rose. A murder suspect on the run, and a killer's target missing. It was a recipe for disaster.

He thought of Denzel. He wasn't much of a dog lover, or lover of most things, beside his wife. He never understood why someone would want the responsibility of a pet. It was something they had to take care of on top of everything else they already had in their lives.

Hicks had a terrible time keeping up with his marriage and, now adult, child. How could he ever take care of an animal that depended on him to live every day?

He had to admit, though, that even for the small time he'd had Denzel in his car, he enjoyed the mutt. For a moment, he wished he could take time away from the hectic night to walk the dog before giving it back to Rina Kent. There was something calming about the dog's presence that he liked.

Perhaps someday he could have a pet of his own, when he hung up his duty belt and gave in his badge.

He thought of Aileen. Hicks thought a lot about retirement now that he was older, but with his wife now out of the picture, what else besides work did he have left to look forward to when he came home? Dogs were a man's best friend, after all. An animal in his apartment could be a good thing for him, Hicks thought.

The radio went off in his patrol car. "Detective Hicks," a voice called out.

"Go ahead," Hicks answered.

"I'm at the Alder scene. You told me to call in if we found anything else."

"And what did you find, officer?"

"There was another set of footprints at the crime scene, sir."

"Right," Hicks said. "The woman, Mrs. Kent, do they belong to her?"

"Negative, sir," the patrol officer answered. "They belong to someone with a larger shoe size. Another update as well. We ran a gun registration search on the names you gave us. Cody Alder, and Marie Deaver. We got a hit. Marie Deaver has a licensed gun that matches the forensics on Adam Greber."

"Really?" Hicks said. "Everything is starting to come together. What about her missing persons case?"

"We closed it after a few weeks. Purchases were made in the Vancouver area. Apparently, she had left a note for her sister as well... just like what was reported."

"Well, looks like we need to keep an eye out for a third person," Detective Hicks said. "Expand our search to include Marie Deaver now. Put out a description for all cars." Hicks clicked with his mouth. "Good work, officer." As soon as the call ended, he called Dispatch. "I need patrol cars sent to two locations. Dr. Rina Kent, and Phyllis Deaver." The detective provided their addresses. "There's a car near Deaver's already."

Two murderers, Hicks thought. Trouble seemed to follow Rina Kent, and Hicks wanted a car near her at all times tonight to ensure there were no more issues from her.

The dispatcher answered after a moment. "Detective, a 911 call was made about twenty minutes ago from someone identifying themselves as Rina Kent. She requested the police go to the home of Phyllis Deaver."

CHAPTER 33

Rina ran as fast as she could to Phyllis's home. After reading the puzzle, she'd demanded the convenience store clerk call 911. Thankfully the clerk hadn't asked too many questions and allowed her the use of the office phone. When she left the store, she realized Phyllis's home wasn't too far from where she was. She left Denzel tied to the post outside the store, petting him once before leaving.

She wasn't sure what she was going to do when she got to Phyllis's home but did not want Denzel with her when she got there.

When she got to Phyllis Deaver's home she walked on the opposite side of the street so as to not trip off any lights along the fence line. Rina spotted a police cruiser on the driveway and smiled. Her happiness didn't last long when she spotted an officer leaving the house.

The officer got into the cruiser and backed out of the driveway until they were off the property. The car drove down the opposite side of the road where Rina was stood watching.

She spotted Phyllis under the porch light watching the cop car until it was down the road and out of sight. Rina realized she was underneath a streetlight and quickly ran into an area of bushes. She peeked through thick leaves until she saw Phyllis go back inside her home.

Did the cop check on Amy? Did the cop search the house or did Phyllis kick him off her property the moment she spotted him? Where was Detective Hicks? She had asked the 911 operator to inform him of what was happening.

Rina would make sure not to be caught as easily this time on Phyllis's property. She ran back down the street until she was on the beach. The waves on the beachfront looked treacherous. Rina followed the fence line until the picket fence climbed along a hill that ended at a small cliff near a rocky section of the beach. With the help of the moon, Rina spotted a floodlight aimed towards the water.

Amy could have meant many things when she wrote down "Aunt Phyllis" on the puzzle, but the answer that made sense was that Phyllis Deaver was the murderer of Adam Greber and Ron Alder. Jonas was missing. Rina knew Amy was in danger.

Rina rolled up her pants until they were above her knees. She wasn't sure how far out she would have to be not to trigger the security lights, but if she could get far enough from the beachfront, she could get to the other side unnoticed and without triggering the security system.

The police might have been satisfied that everything was okay at Phyllis Deaver's residence, but Rina needed to see for herself that Amy was safe.

A light was on in Phyllis's basement. Rina tried to remember the layout. There was only Marie Deaver's room and her daughter's in the basement.

Rina looked out into the dark water. She had hoped once she was closer the waves would seem less intimidating but she'd been wrong. Rina could swim if something happened. She'd nearly got her Lifeguard license when she was a teenager.

A red sign on the beach read: "Beach's Closed. High Current."

Rina calmed herself. She had been to the beach before in Carrington. She swam in lakes, oceans. Bow River didn't worry her. What did was the lack of light.

She took off her shoes and stuffed her socks inside them. She held them in her hands, putting her arms out as if she was a bird, as she took her first step into the cold water.

She immediately felt a chill go through her entire system and shivered. She looked back at Amy's bedroom light before taking a second step.

She talked herself into continuing down the beach, the water rising higher on her body with each step. Even with it above her ankles, she could feel the current. She continued to take step after step, but then a scream stopped her.

Looking back at Phyllis's home, all she heard was the slight night breeze. Until another gut-wrenching scream came from the house.

Rina quickened her pace. She decided she had gone far enough and tried to head towards Phyllis's property. With the next step her foot sank much deeper than expected and Rina nearly fell in the water, her body soaked. Rina found her footing but with the water up above her waist, and the water pressure crushing against her side, she lost her footing and started gliding down the river.

Her arms swung rapidly, and she lost one of her shoes. She tried to swim closer to the shoreline but could barely gain an inch as the water continued to pull her back. She panicked, thinking instantly of stories she had heard of children being sucked into a current and dying. There was an incident last summer where a young child was pulled down the river. The mother had run into the water to save her child but drowned too.

Rina tried to fight the current and push herself towards the shore, but her head fell under the water. She'd thought she was a good swimmer until Mother Nature reminded her she was powerless. Her head went below the water and she was sucked to the bottom. With all the force she could muster she was able to push off the ground using her feet until her head was above water again. Rina let out a scream as she continued to get tossed deeper out into the dark waters.

She spotted the dock she had seen before. At the end of it was the canoe that bobbed on the waves, threatening to slip its mooring. As she got closer, Rina knew it was her last chance before being pushed further out into the river.

She pushed herself until she managed to change her course to float towards the dock. When close enough, she reached out and grabbed on to the jetty, holding tightly. Water gushed against her back, attempting to push her under the dock and through the other side, back into the river. She continued to swim along the side of the dock until one of her feet could touch the bottom.

Rina nearly laughed with happiness at surviving the ordeal when she realized a floodlight on the dock was beaming down at her. Rina looked at Phyllis Deaver's home and saw the light on her porch turn on. Phyllis stepped out onto it, a gun in her hand.

Phyllis started towards the dock. Rina, unsure what to do, put her hand on the underside of the jetty. She could hide underneath, she thought. Her body already felt frozen, and she was shaking. The shadowy figure of Phyllis Deaver came towards her.

She moved her hand along the underside of the dock but felt seaweed between her fingers. She brought her hand quickly back and put it on top of the jetty. She tried to think about what to do with Phyllis coming, until she saw what she was really holding.

Clenched between her index and middle finger was a coil of brown hair. She reached under the dock and felt a large mass floating near her. She pushed it out more and could feel a large chain wrapped around it.

She tried to swing the floating mass towards her. She took another step to get a better grip, and felt it move. The floodlights illuminated a blue torso and the bloated face of a woman. Around her neck was a green emerald necklace.

The woman under the dock was Marie Deaver.

"She always loved my beach." Rina looked up at Phyllis pointing a gun at her. "It felt right to keep her here. Where else could I bring her, really? I didn't want her to die! Even after she was... gone, I took care of Amy. Then you had to find a way to have her talk, communicate. I wanted her to be assigned to you, not Belinda, because I knew how shit you've become at your job. Too bad for you that you're not as bad as everyone thought." She nodded at the beach behind her. "Now... get out."

Rina bobbed her head under the water and went under the dock. Half in the water, she heard the blasts of the gun. Several holes were punched in the jetty around her. She held on tightly to the sides of the dock and made her way down towards the canoe at the end.

Several more shots made her bob her head back under the water. The current started to get stronger as she neared the end. Another shot fired and Rina nearly lost her grip.

When Rina could feel the rope to the canoe, she followed it and put her hand into the boat. Phyllis screamed and fired at her.

"You're not leaving, Dr. Kent!" she barked. Rina could hear her footsteps getting closer. Using what strength she could manage, Rina pushed back down the dock and clung to the side.

When she put her head above water, Phyllis was staring over the other side of the jetty. She smiled when she saw Rina, but it was too late.

Rina managed to push out the paddle she grabbed from the boat. She held on tight to the dock and with the help of the current jammed the paddle blade into Phyllis's midsection. Phyllis yelled as she fell into the water.

Rina attempted to haul herself onto the dock but struggled. Rina clung to the jetty as she watched Phyllis float down the river, screaming. She managed to fire two more shots into the darkness before she was out of sight completely. Although Rina couldn't see her, she could still hear the echoed scream of Phyllis Deaver.

Rina pulled herself up, and managed to get one leg on top and soon after the other. She took a deep, cold breath as she stood up.

Shaking, she ran towards Phyllis's house. She prayed that Amy would be okay. The screams she had heard must have been from her. What had her aunt done?

She ran inside the home, rubbing her soaked torso for warmth. In the living room was a throw blanket that she grabbed and wrapped around her. Rina ran down the hall, towards the stairs.

"Amy!" she called out. "Amy!"

She heard nothing in response.

When she got downstairs, she ran to Amy's door, which was partly open. "Amy!" she called one last time.

She opened the door fully, preparing herself for the worst. She let out a deep breath when she saw Amy sitting crossed-legged on the floor, putting together a puzzle.

"Amy?" Rina said calmly, walking up beside her. "Are you okay?"

Amy quickly glanced up at Rina, smiled and turned back towards her puzzle. She rocked back and forth slowly, humming her song. Rina's smile faded when she saw Amy's bruised right cheek.

"What did your aunt do to you, Amy?" She asked the question without expecting an answer. "I'll be right back. I'm going to call the police."

Amy paid no attention and continued to put together her puzzle.

Rina sighed, knowing that Amy was safe. When she turned, she noticed Marie Deaver's room was open as well. Rina opened the door and screamed. Jonas lay on the bed. Blood pooled around his head, soaking into the white sheets.

"Jonas!" she yelled, running to him, and checking his pulse. "Are you okay?"

Jonas turned his head slightly, a groan escaping his lips when he did. "Rina, is that you?" He attempted to focus his eyes but struggled.

"It's me!" she said. She took off a pillowcase and wrapped it around his head. "What happened?"

Jonas pursed his lips. "My head. I... I'm hurt. I need—"

Rina wrapped her arms around his torso. "I'm calling you

an ambulance!"

CHAPTER 34

Rina watched as paramedics wrapped Jonas's head with gauze in Phyllis's living room. One of them continued to quiz him. Jonas was now fully aware of his surroundings. He didn't complain of light hurting his eyes or a sense of dizziness. The only thing that hurt, he said, was where Phyllis cracked him on the head. He wasn't sure how she did it, he said.

Detective Hicks watched as well. While the paramedics were providing first aid to Jonas, Rina told the detective everything that had led to her being at Deaver's home. She told him where he could find the body of Marie Deaver. She explained how Phyllis fell off the dock and could still be out there. She also told him where to find Denzel.

Hicks made some calls for a crime scene team to come to Phyllis's home and called Alberta Search and Rescue for Phyllis. He even had an officer grab her mutt.

"I don't think she would have made it," Detective Hicks said. "The beaches have been closed all week due to the storms and high current." He shook his head. "I'm still not sure how you could have survived out there."

"Luck," Rina answered. She looked at the picture of Marie and Phyllis in the canoe on the living room wall. Rina turned to Amy, who sat on the other side of the living room with a puzzle.

Detective Hicks saw her concern. "She's okay," he said. "One of the paramedics quickly looked her over. A bad bruise, that's it."

"What kind of a person would do that to her?"

"With your help, we will figure this out with Amy."

"Where will she go?"

"She's over eighteen," Hicks said. "I called a social worker but it's too early in the morning and I haven't heard back yet. I'm sure there's a shelter, or somewhere we can take her. Last resort, I could get a motel room for her."

"She can stay with me," Rina said.

"Isn't that against some sort of rule? A psychiatrist can't have their patients sleep over, right?"

Rina laughed, wrapping the blanket around her. The laugh led to a cough. "I'm no longer her psychiatrist. Also, I may be fired."

Hicks laughed back. "That cough doesn't sound nice. Let's get the paramedics to look you over."

"After they're done with him," she said, nodding at Jonas.

The paramedics looked back at the detective after finishing their assessment of Jonas.

"So," Hicks said, "does he need to go to the hospital?"

A female paramedic answered. "He's okay. We just gave him a pain med. He doesn't appear to have a concussion."

"He does have a large hematoma on the top of his skull," the other paramedic said.

"So, no hospital, I take it?" the detective repeated.

Jonas rubbed his hand against his forehead. "I'd discharge myself from the hospital if I was a patient admitted to the ER." He smiled at the detective. "Just ice and keep an eye on me."

"He can talk to me?" the detective asked the paramedics.

"Detective Hicks," Jonas said, "ask away."

"Well, what the hell are you doing here?"

"Phyllis called me at my home. She told me to come over immediately. She said she had to tell me something about Rina. She said it was important, but we couldn't speak over the phone. She said she wasn't sure if she needed to call the cops on Rina. Phyllis said she had information that could change everything. I had just finished my date, or dinner, with her and I came to Phyllis house immediately after she called."

Rina was confused. "What did she say I did?"

"That's what I wanted to know too," Jonas said. He looked at the detective. "Do you know about the workbook Amy had in her room? The one that Rina took when she came by Phyllis's home?"

Detective Hicks nodded. "Rina came clean with everything as far as I know."

"I was worried about Rina." He looked at her and lowered his head. "She was obsessed with Marie Deaver and her daughter, Amy. When Phyllis said she was going to call the cops about what Rina had supposedly done, I needed to know what it could be. I was worried Rina hadn't told me everything."

"What happened when you arrived?"

"Phyllis told me she needed to show me Marie Deaver's bedroom. She had found something inside the room that she believed Rina put there on purpose when she was over. A letter. I asked her what it was, but Phyllis said she was too distraught by what it said and wanted me to read it. She said she wasn't sure if she should call the cops. I went downstairs and went into the bedroom. Phyllis pointed to the dresser. I went closer to see but then I remember a pain to the back of my head and waking up... to Rina's voice."

Hicks took notes on his pad. "Do you know what she hit you with?"

"No, I don't."

"We found a metal fire poker at the foot of the bed," Hicks said, clicking with the side of his mouth.

"That woman was vile. I knew something was off." Jonas touched the top of his head, rubbing his hand against the gauze. "I paid the price for thinking I could believe her."

"Do you know where Cody Alder could be?"

"No... I don't," Jonas said. "Why?"

Detective Hicks snapped his writing pad closed and placed it back in his inner pocket. "We know there were two killers at Ron Alder's home. We have a strong lead that Cody Alder was one of them. We know the other murderer was Phyllis

Deaver now. We can't find Cody. All three of you are not safe until we can find him."

Jonas took a deep breath. "What happens now?"

"I suggest a motel room," Hicks said. "I can give you a ride to one myself. Make sure your setup is safe. I can arrange for a patrol car to keep watch."

"That sounds like a good plan," Rina said. "We should stay together, Jonas. We can share a room."

Jonas laughed. "Okay."

CHAPTER 35

Detective Hicks

Detective Hicks followed through with his promise.

After Rina grabbed some personal items from her home, he drove all three to a motel for the night, even the mutt. Denzel lay in Rina's lap, his tail whacking Jonas's shoulder in the back seat.

Once they were checked into a room, Hicks gave them some advice for the remainder of the night. Don't leave the room. No phone calls. Stay out of sight until Cody Alder can be found.

"Hopefully, by the end of today we'll have found him," Hicks said. He looked at Jonas. "You're the last person left on this list, Jonas, which means you're in extreme danger."

"I understand," Jonas said. "We won't leave."

"We will be okay," Rina said, holding his side.

Before leaving, Hicks patted Denzel on the head. "It's going to be a busy night," he said to the couple. "Stay safe."

Detective Hicks went back to his cruiser, taking out another cigarette. He'd nearly finished the entire pack in one night. Tomorrow's another day for me to quit, he thought. Tomorrow's another day for me to start again.

Hicks checked in with his patrol men, but there were no new updates on Cody. He drove back to Ron Alder's home. He had time to kill while the crime scene team dealt with Phyllis Deaver's property. He hoped that by going back to the second crime scene, he'd come up with a lead. Something that had been overlooked that could help with the search for Cody.

When Hicks arrived, he parked on the street. The streetlamps were distanced too far from each other to see much of anything around him. When he got out of his car, he looked at the house, and the dark forest behind him. The sound of something rustling in the undergrowth caught his attention. He took out his flashlight and shined it into the woods.

Suddenly he felt very foolish coming to the scene of a murdered father, when the son was still missing. He placed his hand on top of his gun, readying himself as he continued to search the darkness. When he saw a shadowy figure jump, he took out his pistol and nearly fired. He flashed his light at the deer that continued to jump until it was out of sight and back in the woods.

Hicks laughed, patting his jacket pocket. He sighed when he remembered he'd smoked the whole pack in only a few hours. Aileen would be proud, he knew.

Hicks walked up the pathway to the front door, ducking under the police tape. He unlocked it and went inside slowly. The room was dark, as forensics had left it after processing the home for evidence.

Hicks stepped around the marked evidence on the floor, making his way to the couch where the body was found. All that was left behind were several taped off areas with evidence markings.

Hicks looked around the dark room with his flashlight. He flashed it into the kitchen area. He was becoming more paranoid in his old age. He smiled to himself. Dark rooms were starting to bother him.

His cell phone rang loudly, cutting the silence, the high-pitched song he'd chosen for a ringtone almost hurting his ears.

"Hicks," he barked into the receiver.

"It's Rina."

"What's up?"

"Adam Greber, I forgot to mention this, but he kept files at his home."

"Okay," Hicks said, not understanding the urgency of her call.

"Marie Deaver's file could be there from her time at the hospital," she said, her voice strained.

"They let you keep patient files at your home after you've retired?"

"Adam Greber was still involved on some committees, and other charity events at the hospital," Rina said. "It's possible that because of his ongoing involvement, even though it was small, that he still has records. I tried calling Sarah Alloy to confirm this, but she didn't answer."

"Probably because it's four in the morning," Hicks said with a sneer. "Are you listening to what I asked of you?"

"That's it from me. You won't hear from me again tonight."

"I'll give you an update tomorrow. I need to catch some shut-eye at some point too. I'll be at the motel in the afternoon."

Rina thanked him and he terminated the call. He continued to search the home for clues. He was astounded by how few personal items Mr. Alder had in his home. There were no photos on the wall, or anywhere else he could find, only expensive artwork.

Besides the leather couches and smell of cigars in each room, you wouldn't know anything about who lived here.

Hicks went into the main bedroom. Crime scene had found a blood trail that started in this room and led down the stairs. They concluded the killers had surprised Alder in his bedroom and forced him to the living room, where he was ultimately killed.

Even in his bedroom, he could find nothing personal, not even a porno magazine. He stepped into a closet nearly the size of Hicks's bedroom. A rack of suits was on one side, and across were shirts and jeans. A bottom rack was dedicated to expensive-looking shoes. A tie rack was filled with fine prints and materials.

A fishing rod lay in an area of the closet that was bare of clothes. Above on one of the built-in shelves was a stuffed bass attached to a plank of wood. The trophy wasn't hung up. Hicks picked it up and looked at it.

Beside the fish was a picture of Ron and Cody Alder, who looked much younger. At the bottom was a metal plaque that was inscribed: "05-08-2014. Carster Point. Cody's first fish".

Hicks wasn't much of an outdoors person but had heard of the spot from colleagues on the force who enjoyed fly fishing. He looked at the smiling faces of father and son, putting his radio to his mouth.

"Dispatch," he said. "This is Detective Hicks. Have a car search Carster Point for Cody Alder." Dispatch came back and confirmed they would do so. Hicks took his time searching the remainder of the home but could not find anything out of the ordinary that could allude to where Cody could be hiding. He switched off the lights and locked up on his way out.

He drove back to Phyllis Deaver's home. He walked across the beach, lights from Deaver's property lighting up as he made his way to the dock. A group of investigators had pulled Marie Deaver's body from the rapid waters onto a blue tarp on top of the sand.

"What are we thinking?" he asked.

One of the crime scene investigators with a goatee looked at him. "She's been dead for weeks. The body was badly decomposed. How did you even identify it?"

"The woman who found her," Hicks said. "She identified the necklace she was wearing. What do we know of the cause of death?"

"There are multiple stab wounds to her torso. You can see entry wounds all over her ripped dress. The cuts seem deep, but not enough to have killed her instantly. My guess is that when she was brought to the dock and put in the water, she was still alive, maybe barely, but alive."

"What a night."

"Do you have a motive from the witness?"

"I still don't have much," he said. No motive. A second killer still on the loose. A list of names down to just Jonas Kent.

Why did Amy Deaver say the four names? Adam Greber, Ron Alder, Phyllis Deaver and Jonas Kent. How could they be connected? Nothing was making any sense. Hicks took out his pack of cigarettes and sighed when he discovered it was empty.

"Do you have a cig?" the detective asked the forensics team. All of them gestured that they didn't.

"Hell. Going to be a long night indeed." Hicks nodded and made a few notes on his pad. "Let me know if you have any new updates throughout the night." He trudged back down the beach, and his cell phone rang again. "Hicks."

"We found him, sir," a patrol officer shouted into the phone. "He's covered in blood."

"Cody Alder?" Hicks exclaimed. "Where are you?"

CHAPTER 36

After Detective Hicks left the archaic motel room, Rina took her time looking around. Although it was the year 2022, the motel room was permanently stuck in the 1980s. The wood panel walls made the two bedrooms seem much smaller than they were.

Jonas shuffled to the couch, plopping himself on it. A musty smell hit Rina's nostrils, making her wince when he sat. "I'll take the couch," he said, rubbing the side of his head.

Rina shook her head. "No way. You're on the bed. You need a good rest. Amy can take the other bed." Rina sat on the couch, smelling the dusty aroma again. "I'll take this."

Jonas got up, taking his time. "Well, I know better than to argue with you."

Rina guided Amy to her bed. "It will be okay," she comforted her. "Tomorrow we will figure everything out." She turned to the table, grabbing a puzzle box. "Here," she said, giving it to Amy. "Something to soothe you in our new room for the night. You can work on the puzzle, and we can hopefully all try and sleep soon. We can get you another journal tomorrow too."

Jonas was already laid out on the bed, breathing heavily. Denzel jumped and lay on his other side. Rina stood watching him. "I'm fine," he said, opening one eye. "I don't have a concussion. I can sleep, Rina, it's okay. It's been a night. I'm exhausted."

Rina agreed. She turned off the lights in the room, leaving

a bedroom lamp near Amy's bed so she could continue to work on her puzzle. She lay on the couch, staring at the ceiling. She tried to close her eyes but could only manage to do so for a few minutes at a time.

After ten minutes she got up and reminded Amy that it was time to sleep. She turned off the light and sat on the bed beside her. "I'm sorry, Amy," she said softly. "I'm sure tonight was hard on you. You're safe now." She thought of the body that floated under Phyllis Deaver's dock. The corpse of Amy's mother.

Did Amy have any idea what had happened to her? Did she have an understanding of how much danger she was in tonight, or that her mother's body had been discovered?

Amy sat on top of the bed sheets, rocking slowly. Rina put a hand to the side of her head. "You're safe now," she repeated. It was as if she had to remind herself as well.

Rina worried what would happen with Amy. What type of facility would they bring her to? Who would pay for it? What type of care would she receive? After everything Amy Deaver had gone through, she deserved to be treated well.

Marie Deaver had a vision of what she wanted for her daughter; it made Rina sad to think her goal would never be achieved. Everyone that could care for Amy was dead. Who would help her?

Amy put the puzzle pieces into the box and handed it to Rina. She slid under the sheets and stared at the ceiling.

"Goodnight," Rina said, leaving her in the bed. When she stood up, she turned and saw Jonas was already snoring. She envied how her husband could rest peacefully after what had happened.

Rina lay back on the couch, taking a blanket she had found in the motel closet and wrapping it around her torso. Rina hadn't realized how small the couch was. Her feet dangled off the side, making it harder for her to find a comfy spot to sleep.

Sleep was the last thing she could do, she thought. Instead, she ran through the day's events as if it were a movie in her head. She imagined that she should be breaking down and crying after surviving a near drowning, finding several bodies, and Phyllis shooting at her. She assumed she would have some type of emotion after pushing Phyllis into the water.

None of Phyllis's and Cody Alder's actions made sense. Amy had a list of names. Now three out of four of those names were dead. Jonas was the last one alive. Why did Amy have the list of names to begin with? Why did Phyllis and Cody start to kill the people on the list? Why was Phyllis Deaver one of those names?

Rina stared at the ceiling, looking for answers. Instead, all she had were more questions.

She thought of Adam Greber. Marie Deaver was a patient of his. That was the only connection as far as Rina knew. Because the records were confidential you needed a password to open them at the hospital. Dr. Greber was old school though. He liked having paper copies of records and kept many at home.

Marie Deaver's file could still be there.

Rina carefully stood up from the couch. She peered over at Amy, who was now sound asleep in her bed. She could still hear Jonas's snoring. Even Denzel appeared to be fully out of it. Rina took out her cell phone and quietly opened the door, stepping outside.

Rina looked out into the dark night and a near-empty parking lot. Lightning streaked across the sky, illuminating the road. She typed in Detective Hicks's number and called.

"Hicks," he barked into the receiver.

"It's Rina."

"What's up?"

"Adam Greber, I forgot to mention this, but he kept files at his home."

"Okay," Hicks said, not understanding the urgency of her call.

"Marie Deaver's file could be there from her time at the hospital," she said, her voice strained. Hicks continued to sound grouchy. Rina got the impression he would look into it eventually, even though Rina felt there could be important information in the file.

"I'll give you an update tomorrow," Hicks said. "I need to catch some shut-eye at some point too. I'll be at the motel in the afternoon."

Rina got off the phone hoping to have heard a better update from the detective. She went back inside and quietly pulled the blanket over herself on the couch. She looked over at Jonas's bed where Denzel was sitting up, his ears perked.

"Back to bed, Denzel," Rina said to him, and he lay back down. She attempted to close her eyes, at some point falling asleep for a moment, only to wake up wondering what was happening. She looked at her phone. She had been attempting to sleep for nearly thirty minutes. Even worse, there were no updates from Detective Hicks.

Would Hicks go to Adam Greber's home like Rina recommended? They could be searching all night for Cody.

What if Cody found them at the motel? She tried to calm herself, knowing he wouldn't think to come to a motel with a near-empty parking lot. Detective Hicks dropped them off. Her personal car wasn't here. It would be impossible for Cody to know they were staying there.

On the nightstand beside her was the television remote. She turned on the power and waited for the television to turn on. Just as the rest of the items in the room were from a different era, the television seemed like it needed a few seconds to warm up before powering on.

She flicked through a few channels until a news channel popped up. "Breaking news! An investigation into Holy Saints—" Rina turned off the television. The last thing she wanted was to watch what had happened to them tonight unfold on the news.

She quietly stood up from the couch again.

"Are you okay?" Rina turned and saw Jonas sitting up in his bed. "Do you want to lay down with me?"

Rina smiled. "I do, but I just need to... go for a walk. Clear my mind."

"You need sleep."

"I work midnights," Rina reminded him. "I'm fine."

"You haven't slept since yesterday."

"I'll walk around the block. I'm fine." Denzel perked up on the bed when Rina said the word "walk." "Back to bed," she whispered to her dog. She looked at Jonas. "You too."

"Don't stay out too long," he said, turning over.

Rina looked over at Amy and smiled again. She took another look at Jonas, her smile fading. Why were you on the list? she thought to herself.

Rina quietly stepped outside. She peered around the empty downtown streets of Carrington. She began walking.

If someone was to ask her where she was going, she would act coy, and say she was wandering aimlessly. That wasn't the real answer.

Adam Greber could have files in his home that could answer the questions keeping her up at night. Rina needed to know.

Rina strode down the empty street. Greber's home was only a few blocks away from the motel. A car took a right from an alley and headed towards her. Rina panicked for a moment, until it passed her.

I should listen to what Detective Hicks told me for a change, she thought. The idea of attempting to sleep when so much was unanswered seemed unimaginable.

All she wanted to do was hold Jonas until he felt better and fly away with him to a beach somewhere. Rekindle their marriage. Pretend the last six months never happened.

But they did happen. Jonas kissed another woman. Now he's on a list full of dead people. A list that Amy Deaver brought with her to the psych ward.

Rina continued to hurry down the street until she spotted Adam Greber's home. It was a modest house, unlike Phyllis's or Ron Alder's. A regular sized home, with no garage and a large front porch with two chairs facing the street.

With no vehicle in the driveway or close to the home, Rina was certain Adam Greber's wife was not there.

Why would someone stay by themselves in the home where their husband was murdered? She knew Greber had two adult children. His wife, Veronica, likely was with one of them.

Rina recalled the dream she'd had of the home. It looked nothing like what she'd created in her sleep.

There was no police tape on the front door. It looked like the rest of the homes down the street. It was as if nothing out of the ordinary had happened just a few nights ago.

Before approaching it, she looked at the windows for any movement inside but saw nothing. Rina glanced around the neighborhood and saw the same. Nothing. The streetlights illuminated the empty street, and a plastic bag rolled across the road in the breeze. Lightning streaked the night sky.

If Jonas was awake, he would likely start worrying about her, Rina knew. Part of her cried out for her to leave and go back to him, Denzel... and Amy. Whatever files Adam Greber had on Marie Deaver, if any, would come to light eventually.

That wasn't good enough for Rina, though.

She climbed the cement steps and attempted to open the door, but it was locked. She suspected it wouldn't be that easy. Rina walked over to the large windows that led into Greber's dining area and living room. In the dark she made out yellow-colored tents that read "Evidence". Rina knew in her heart Veronica must not be home when she saw the dark red stain that was beneath the yellow marking.

Rina saw which window could open from peering inside and attempted to slide it up. It nudged an inch before stopping. Rina cursed under her breath and stared out into the quiet neighborhood. Many of the homes had large porches with seating on them, but thankfully nobody was out at this time. They would have had a fun show watching an adult woman break into her former boss's house.

Rina went back down the steps and along the side of the home, attempting to open windows on the way. She'd nearly given up when a window into a room on the main floor of the house nudged further than the rest. With another shove, she managed to open it fully.

Rina jumped and pushed her body through the opening. Once inside the room, she used her cellphone as a flashlight. Several photos of Adam Greber with his family at different times in their lives hung on the wall. On the other side hung his diplomas from university, along with certificates, awards and achievements. A large desk was to one side of the room, along with several bookcases.

Rina realized she had managed to not only break into Adam Greber's home but his home office. She took her time sorting through the room, attempting to find any files that he took home with him. She opened the desk drawers first but found nothing out of the ordinary.

She opened a large cardboard box under the desk, but it only contained tax information from the last several years. Rina flashed her phone around the bookcases, opening any containers she found. On the last shelf, near the bottom, was another cardboard box. She opened it and was thrilled when the first document had the Holy Saints symbol on it.

She sorted through the files. Thankfully, Adam was organized. Many items were alphabetized. Rina's heart fluttered when she saw the name she was looking for.

Deaver, Marie.

Rina grabbed the file folder out of the box and opened it to the first page. Holy Saints Psychiatric Ward intake Report. Patient's name: Marie Deaver.

She began reading the report, letting the words sink in as she did. The report read:

Marie Deaver presents herself to the ward with suicidal ideation. She arrived at Holy Saints Emergency Room demanding to speak with a psychiatrist directly, and not an emergency physician. The patient reports an increase of depression symptoms she says she has experienced for over six months. At the heart of her concerns is the behaviour of an ex-boyfriend. After termination of their relationship, the patient says she has been harassed and stalked by her ex-boyfriend. She reports he leaves her distressing letters about him wanting to be with her sexually. "Needs her body," was a line from his most recent letter left on her doorstep, she explained.

Rina looked up from the report, remembering the note she found on Phyllis Deaver's fire mantel. That letter was addressed to Phyllis though, not Marie. Rina continued reading:

The patient says when she leaves her home, the ex-boyfriend will coincidentally be at the same place. One time she reportedly yelled at him in public when she found him talking to her daughter after she left her alone to go to the bathroom at the local library, where she homeschools her daughter. She suspects that he is harassing her and her daughter outside their home at night. He will knock on her window, and at times her daughter's as well. By the time the police arrive, he leaves. She has reported him to the police, but they advise they are not able to arrest him as there is no concrete evidence it is him outside her home at night.

The patient says she has gone to extremes such as to purchase a gun, and live temporarily with her sister, Phyllis Deaver. The writer must note that Phyllis Deaver is a pediatrician at Holy Saints Hospital.

The writer must also report that the patient has named another staff member at Holy Saints as the ex-boyfriend harassing her. She reports that—

Lightning Illuminated the room, and the area outside the window. Rina looked up when she saw someone standing outside, staring back at her through the glass.

CHAPTER 37

Detective Hicks

Hicks parked in front of Carster Point fishing spot, beside several police cruisers. As soon as he stepped out of his vehicle, he heard Cody yelling.

"Get away from me! Get away, pigs!"

Hicks hurried down towards the dock. Several planks were missing, with a large gap near the end where Cody Alder yelled at the police officers attempting to talk to him.

Lightning streaked across the sky, illuminating the young man, and the dark flowing waters behind him. Cody had on white scrubs stained almost entirely red. He gripped a small pocketknife, pointing it towards the officers.

"We just want to talk," one of the cops yelled back.

Hicks hurried along the jetty, careful to watch his footing on the decrepit planks. Hicks was not a swimmer by any means, and given how far out from the shore they were he knew he wouldn't stand a chance in the water.

"Cody!" Hicks yelled once close enough. He patted the shoulders of the officers as he slid between them. "I'm Detective Hicks." Rain started to fall from the sky. Hicks wiped his face.

"I know who you are," the son yelled back. "I don't want to talk to you or your men! I just want... to not be here anymore." He turned towards the waters. "This is it for me. I don't care anymore."

"Drowning is a terrible way to go," Hicks said. "That's how

your partner went out. The fire service informed me they found the body of Phyllis Deaver not too far from here."

Cody raised an eyebrow at him. "What?"

"Why did you kill your father?" Hicks asked. "Why? Just tell us. We need to understand what happened."

"I didn't kill them!" he shouted.

"Adam Greber!" Hicks yelled. "Why? Why did you make a list of names?"

Cody didn't respond. He turned around fully to the water ahead of him, not acknowledging Hicks at all.

"I failed him," he said looking back at Hicks. "He never told me I did, but I knew I wasn't what he wanted. A nurse? He wanted me to be a doctor. I failed him. He had enough decency, not to tell me. Hell, he rarely spoke to me, really."

"Is that why you did it?" Hicks asked. He stepped closer, looking down at the missing planks he would have to step over to get to Cody.

"Step back!" Cody yelled at the detective. "Let me be at peace! Let me do something right." Cody turned back to the end of the dock, his feet half over the edge. He opened his arms wide and took a step.

Hicks immediately jumped across the gap and grabbed onto the back of his white shirt, pulling back forcefully. Cody still fell into the water, but Hicks gripped his shirt.

Once in the water, Cody threw his hands frantically, and managed to grab one of the jetty's piles. "Help me!" he shrieked.

"What the hell did you go in there for, kid?" Hicks muttered, attempting to keep him from drifting off into the water. "Give me your hand!"

Another officer jumped across the missing planks and helped Hicks pull Cody back on top of the dock. Hicks escorted him down the jetty as he shivered.

"I just want the pain to stop!" Cody said, tears streaming down his face.

Detective Hicks pulled his handcuffs from his belt and placed Cody's arms behind his back. "You are under arrest for the murder of Ron Alder," he said cuffing one hand. "You have the right to resin silent—"

"I didn't kill my father," Cody said calmly. "I found him that way. I... couldn't handle it. I'm better now. I—"

"Let me finish," Hicks said, cuffing his other hand. "Anything you say can and will be used against you in a court of law." Hicks finished reading his Charter rights. He nodded to another officer. "Take him to headquarters for now. Get him a blanket too, and a change of clothes once he's there. Collect his clothes as evidence." The officer began to escort the son to his cruiser when Cody pushed and shoved him with his shoulder.

"I'm better now!" he yelled again. The officer grabbed him forcefully and pulled him to the cruiser, locking him in the back seat.

Hicks nodded at the others. "Good work, boys. Now, go home, for those who are on overtime. Get some rest."

The officer that put Cody Alder into the cruiser came up to Hicks. "Should I keep him in an interview room for you?"

"I'll be there soon. I just want to make a stop. Collect some evidence at one of the crime scenes. Could give us something useful when I talk to the young man."

Another officer approached Hicks with a phone in his hand. "I've got a major crimes unit on the phone, sir," he said. "They said they've been trying to reach you for the past thirty minutes."

"Been a busy night, kid," he said to the cop. "Just grab their name, and I'll chat with him soon."

The officer shoved the phone closer. "They said it's an emergency."

Hicks took it. He wasn't sure what Major Crimes would want from him this early in the morning, but he knew one thing... he wasn't going to sleep anytime soon.

"Hicks here."

"This is Detective Rydell from Major Crimes."

"What can I do for you this fine morning, detective?" he asked, clicking with his mouth.

"We have a breaking case. I was told it involved people from an active case of yours. It's already all over the media. It's a huge fraud case."

"Fraud?" Hicks repeated.

"That's right. A large amount of embezzled money from the new hospital funds. We just started our investigation prompted by the media, but there's four people we're investigating. All of them work at the hospital. Phyllis Deaver, Adam Greber, Ron Alder, and—"

"And Jonas Kent," Hicks finished. "You have my full attention, detective."

CHAPTER 38

"Jonas!" Rina called out. "What are you doing?"

Jonas clenched his fist. He put his hand inside the room and pulled himself in to stand in front of her. His face was blank, devoid of emotion.

"What do you have in your hand?" he asked.

Rina immediately understood that her ex-husband knew what it was. "It was you? Why?"

"I did it for you," he answered solemnly. "I do everything for you, for *us*."

"I never wanted you to kill anyone." Rina attempted to run into the living room, but Jonas grabbed her and forced her to the floor. He laid on top of her, breathing on her face.

"Money!" he exclaimed. "We needed money. After what happened with that girl who killed herself in front of you, you were an entirely different person. I wanted us to leave. Leave here! We could have started fresh. I was chosen to be part of a special committee, along with a few others. We were basically given a blank cheque from management for spending on the new hospital. Ron approached us about a scam. How we could steal money from the funding. We each had to agree fully to the fraud."

"You're hurting me," Rina said. Jonas sat up, still on her midsection, staring down at her.

"You hurt me! I took part in the scam for you! For us!"

"The others," Rina said, out of breath. "Who were they?"

"You already know, don't be stupid! Phyllis Deaver, Adam

Greber and Ron Alder. It was Ron's idea! Not mine. I just went along with it. We could have gone anywhere, any country for that matter! I know you didn't want to be in mental health after the suicide of that girl. Well, what about me? I'm tired of being a doctor, too! The stress I have from lack of sleep. The lack of compassion from the patients I give my life to every day! The families of patients who give me shit! The media who crap on health care professionals! It's not right, Rina. On top of that we had to rack up huge sums of student debt that we're still paying and I'm over thirty! We could have had a better life, somewhere else, doing something else. But no, you didn't want that. You focused on your job more than ever after that girl killed herself. You stopped caring about me! About my needs as a man. You barely kissed me for months. I have a moment of weakness with a pretty nurse, and you leave me?"

"Please," Rina cried out, trying to shift him off her. He didn't budge.

"Please?" He scoffed. "Even after we separated, I still pursued you. I loved you! I would have done anything to have you back."

"Marie Deaver," Rina whispered. "You dated her. You harassed her."

He waved a finger at her. "Don't start. That was before us. Before I met you. I loved her too. I would have done anything for Marie, or her daughter. Even after we split, and she eventually started dating that crooked piece of shit Alder, I still would have helped her."

"You killed her."

Jonas put a hand around her neck and squeezed lightly. "Don't say that! I did not. Marie found out about the scam. She wanted a piece of what we took. She was dating Ron at the time. She tried to extort from us the money that we had stolen! Ron was livid. One night we were having a meeting at Phyllis's house about how we could collect the money without it being traced back to us. We already had the money! She came upstairs and confronted us, demanding her part. She said she was going to go to the cops. She had her phone in her hand, and had already dialed a 9 and a 1."

"What did you do to her?"

Jonas looked back at Rina, his eyes cold. His touch, that she'd once found comforting, even colder. He loosened his grip around Rina's neck. "Nothing! It was Phyllis. She grabbed a fire poker and struck her in the head. Her own sister! We heard Amy walking up the stairs. Ron ran to the kitchen and grabbed a knife. Phyllis demanded he put it back. Nobody was going to hurt her niece. She has an intellectual disability. She's mute, we thought. She ran and grabbed Amy before she saw what happened to her mother. She took care of Amy and Ron Alder finished the job on Marie. There was nothing I could have done to save her. I wanted to! Adam and I dragged her body to the dock and chained her to the bottom of it. We didn't know what else to do. Him and I, we're doctors, not murderers. We couldn't let her body wash ashore somewhere."

"Why did Amy know your names?" Rina asked, confused.

"Marie. It must have been Marie. She must have given her our names. I didn't know the girl could talk. Or write for that matter. Phyllis had kept that from us. I still wouldn't have wanted to harm the girl. Ron found out about her ability to write in a workbook. He ripped out pages from a journal, burnt them and several others he found in the girl's bedroom. Then him and Adam tried to kill her. They spiked her drink with what he thought was a deadly amount of Tylenol. Phyllis watched her camera footage, which confirmed everything. When Amy was found she was barely alive. I saved her at the hospital that night. Marie would have been happy! Phyllis got to Adam Greber first and got him to confirm everything that happened. He told him that Ron Alder was behind it all!"

"You could have gone to the police."

Jonas's empathetic stare vanished. "And give up what we had done? And give back the money? Go to jail? I couldn't accept that. Phyllis neither. We took care of Ron Alder together. I did that one for Marie Deaver, not just for Amy. Before he died, Ron told us management had been warned of a police investigation. The embezzled money had been discovered somehow. The police would figure things out eventually. I hoped we would be long gone by then. Our second chance at our honeymoon. I hoped once we were there you could see that there was nothing more for us in Carrington. We could move to a different country. Live the rest of our lives in love. We had to kill Ron though. He would have gone to the police." Rina turned away from him. With his hand he forced her to stare back at him. "Don't be sad for that piece of garbage. He deserved it for what he did to Marie and what he tried to do to Amy." Jonas smiled. "Don't you see? I care just as much as you do about the girl. She has nobody now to take care of her. We could do that together. We could leave, tonight, with Amy. Leave Canada. Give Amy the life Marie Deaver wanted to provide her. I have the money to do it now."

"You hurt her. Amy. Her face. The bruise. You and Phyllis were going to kill her."

"That was Phyllis. I tried to talk her out of it. You being able to communicate with Amy changed everything. I tried to tell Phyllis it wasn't going to be a problem. The girl isn't capable of telling the police what actually happened. She wouldn't exactly be a creditable witness if she could! I was trying to talk Phyllis out of it when she struck her niece. Then the floodlights on the dock went off and we heard your screams. When I saw you come back from the beach alone, I knew something had happened to Phyllis. I struck myself. And waited."

"What did you do to Cody Alder? He's missing too."

"Nothing," Jonas said, looking away.

"The police think he committed the murders. Why do they think that?"

"I may have placed some evidence to help them look in that direction. He was going to be our fall guy, for everything. That was Phyllis's idea too."

Rina's eyes teared. She thought of the letter on Phyllis's mantel. "You were with Phyllis too? I saw what you wrote to her."

Jonas lowered his head. "I was alone after you left me. I

had no one. She was a mistake. I meant what I said when I said I haven't cared for anyone after you. I was with Phyllis physically, not emotionally. We weren't even together at the time! I would do anything for you." Jonas stood up and offered her a hand.

Rina reluctantly grabbed it and stood up.

"I would do anything for you, but you won't for me," he said, his eyes watering. He grabbed Rina's hand. "It's evident now that I care more about you then you ever did for me!" He dragged her out of the bedroom and into a bathroom across the hall. He opened a medicine cabinet and grabbed a bottle, then dragged Rina to the living room.

He shoved Rina to the couch and opened the pill bottle. "I thought at one time you would do anything for me. Then that girl killed herself. You showed me how much more you cared for your patients than us. How much do you really care for them?" He dropped the pill bottle on her lap. "Acetaminophen. Extra strength. I want to see you take the full bottle."

Rina looked up at him in shock. "No," she whispered.

"It's not going to get better from here, Rina. Do it, and I'll spare Amy. I promise I won't hurt her. It was never my idea to hurt her. I'll keep my promises! Unlike you with our marriage vow. For better or for worse! A Tylenol overdose seems fitting for you. You are killing yourself in your former mentor's living room. That can work. Do it, now!" Rina stood up and attempted to strike him, but he grabbed her hands and held her tightly. "I'll just kill you and the girl next," he said. "Take them and save your patient. Or are you as selfish with your last minutes of life as you've been through our marriage?"

Rina grabbed the bottle and put a pill in her mouth. She waited a moment, waiting for Jonas to change his mind before swallowing.

"You don't need water, Rina," he said with a smile. Rina swallowed the pill and put another to her mouth. "Good!"

Rina noticed movement outside the front window. The red glow of a cigarette moving closer to the front door. Even in the dim light she could make out the large figure holding it.

Detective Hicks reached for his gun and took it out, pointing it at Jonas.

"Swallow it!" Jonas demanded.

Rina sat on the couch and stared up at Jonas, swallowing the pill. She grabbed another and held it to her mouth.

"Don't prolong this, Rina!" Jonas shouted. "I can still change my mind."

Rina gave a thin smile. "The worst thing I did was change my mind… about you! You're a cheater! Stalker! Murderer!"

Jonas smacked the pill bottle from Rina's hand, and yelled at her, reaching out towards her. Rina heard shouting from outside followed by a loud crash of glass. The front window shattered, and Jonas fell to the ground screaming in pain.

CHAPTER 39

Three Months Later

Rina stepped into her home, wiping the sweat from her forehead. She barely ran with Denzel, or ever, and just walked most days. Rina imagined she'd gained at least fifteen pounds in the past few months. The weight made her look fuller, she was told. When she had met up with Sarah for coffee to discuss her return-to-work last week, her boss was happy to see how healthy she looked.

Amy remained at the dining table working on a new puzzle. In the past few months the young woman had lived with Rina, she had purchased many puzzles, especially the ones where they could communicate with each other.

It took some time but slowly Amy would allow Rina to write in her new journal, instead of using puzzles. Rina would write using a green pen, Amy a blue one.

Amy didn't talk about what happened with her mother, or her aunt. Rina didn't bring it up either.

At times when they were watching television and a news update would come up talking about Jonas's court case, Rina would quickly change the channel. It wasn't something she or Amy were interested in knowing more about.

Rina was getting ready for a partial shift that afternoon. Sarah had wanted Rina to wait until after Jonas's conviction before returning to work but Rina refused. She had taken much longer than she wanted off work and was eager to get back to the ward. Sarah reluctantly agreed. She had already worked for the past two weeks and was enjoying being back.

Rina had started therapy after what happened, overcoming her guilt at being a psychiatrist who needed therapy. Even though Jonas would be at court today to answer for his crimes, Rina could care less about the outcome. She had already felt freed of the emotional trauma of everything that happened the past nine months. She didn't only talk about Jonas, but Jenny Berange too.

The story was all over the media. Rina was flooded with phone calls for interview requests, as well as Amy. She turned all of them down.

The hospital gained media attention, and with private donors they were able to recover the embezzled funds and continue with the grand opening of the new hospital, which would be in a month.

Rina was ready for a change. She knew Amy was ready for it as well. Rina had been talking with a local non-profit group who found permanent housing for adults with intellectual disabilities. Amy would be taking a tour of a group home next week to see if it was a good fit for her and the other roommates she would have. There would be a trial period where Amy would live there part-time, and eventually move in full-time. Rina smiled, looking at Amy putting together the puzzle at the kitchen table. Both of them would be easing into life again. Rina would help Amy as much as needed until she was comfortable with the transition.

To be honest, having Amy stay with her after everything had helped. Even though Amy wasn't capable of vocalizing it, Rina felt Amy felt the same. Rina would miss her, but knew it was time for her ex-patient to move onto the next step of her life.

A hard knock on the front door startled her and caused Denzel to stand up, barking insanely. Rina smiled when she saw Detective Hicks at the door. She welcomed him inside, and offered him a coffee, which he declined.

"I just wanted to check in with you," he said, making a

clicking sound. "You weren't in the courtroom today."

"I wanted to move on from everything. You said it was okay I didn't come. Did everything go well?"

Hicks nodded. "He pleaded guilty, just as his lawyers told the prosecutor he would. No surprises for a change. The next step for him is sentencing, which we don't have a date for yet. He's going to remain in prison while that happens, don't worry."

"I'm not. Thanks for checking on me." Rina thought of Jonas, and the night she found out who he really was. "He tried to tell me he killed Adam Greber and Ron Alder to protect Amy. He tried to make himself a hero."

Hicks scoffed. "Maybe that was the reason they told each other to go through with it. Taking their portions of the money they stole likely played a role. How's Amy?" he asked, looking at the young woman completing her puzzle.

"She's fine," Rina said. "I'm going to run out of places to buy her new puzzles."

Hicks laughed. "Well, my wife loves them too. I'm sure I could talk her into decluttering the house and give them to you."

"Thanks. I didn't know you were married," she said, surprised.

"Over thirty years now, with some breaks in between," he said with a smirk. "Just so you know, I'm retiring at the end of the month. They may assign a temporary detective to keep working with you if needed."

"Congratulations," Rina said.

"Thanks," Hicks said. "Over twenty-five years on the job with no breaks. Feels like time for a permanent breakup."

"Any retirement plans?"

Hicks shook his head. "Quality time with Aileen, my wife, my granddaughter. Maybe a dog," he said looking at Denzel. "I'm sure the next detective after me will ask you more about this, but they still can't find any of the money. Not a penny of the dollars that were taken. We looked where Jonas told us to. They searched the homes and properties of all four of them. Do you have any information that could help?"

"Not a clue. What about Cody Alder?"

"He left town almost immediately after being released from jail. We're trying to track him down to ask more questions. He's off the radar for now. I'm sure he will show up again, but that won't be my problem, or yours now."

"Something I wonder now and then, when I think about that night. Cody, he told me he wouldn't say a word. It seemed like he knew about the list in Amy's journal."

"He did. When we questioned him, we found out you weren't the only one who read her journal. He was also trying to figure out why his father was on the list when he found him dead."

Rina took in a deep breath. She wished she hadn't brought it up now. It was better to let go of those terrible memories and move on.

"Thanks again for coming," she said.

Hicks waved bye to Amy and nodded at Rina. He swung the door open and turned to Rina. "Any chance you have a cigarette?"

She made a clicking sound from the side of her mouth. "Nope, sorry."

After Hicks left, Rina prepared herself for her noon shift at Holy Saints. When she arrived at the hospital she was greeted by Sarah and Belinda in the rec room. Part of Rina felt guilty that she wasn't yet working full-time hours. She could tell the heavy caseload had been difficult for her colleagues to manage while she was away.

"How's things?" she asked.

Belinda widened her eyes. "What a busy day. We had three new patients today."

Sarah nodded. "We're just glad to have you back, Rina."

"I was hoping I could possibly start working full-time before the new hospital opens."

"We can talk about that," Sarah said with a smile. "Let's have a quick meeting in my office."

Belinda followed Sarah in, and Rina shut the door behind

her. Sarah sat behind her desk. The other two sat facing her. Rina grabbed a notebook, ready to take notes.

"It's really busy," Sarah said. "Today we got three new patients. Each of them is... very difficult. These are not going to be easy patients to work with. I know our caseloads are busy, but I want to ask for volunteers for—"

"I'll take all three," Rina said, raising her hand.

❉ ❉ ❉

Rina arrived home after working only a few hours. Before leaving, Sarah had agreed to push her schedule so she would be on regular hours within two weeks. Sarah made it clear, though, there would be no more straight midnight shifts, which Rina was happy to agree to.

Rina hung her jacket in the closet and called out to Amy. "I'm back!" Amy didn't answer back of course, but she could hear her humming her song at the kitchen table.

She noticed a large brown stain on the carpet. She looked at the bottom of her shoes, but they were clean. She turned her head and saw multiple footprints leading to the kitchen.

"Amy?' she called out. "Where did you go?"

The mud stains ended where Amy sat at the kitchen table. Rina's shovel leaned against the kitchen doorframe, wet mud on the metal blade.

She looked at Amy, who had a dirt on her face. "Are you okay?"

Amy smiled and rocked back and forth, humming her song. She had put together the puzzle, staining the pieces as well. Rina hadn't realized there was a black, stained duffle bag on the other side of Amy. She pulled the bag closer to her, unzipping it.

Inside were stacks of cash, bundled together. It was filled

to the top.

     Rina looked at Amy.

     Amy glanced up at her, grinned and moved her attention back to her puzzle. "Don't say a word," she whispered.

Note from the author:

I truly hope you enjoyed reading my story as much as I did creating it. As an indie author, what you think of my book is all I care about.

If you enjoyed my story, please take a moment to leave your review on the Amazon store. It would mean the world to me.

Thank you for reading, and I hope you join me next time.

Download My Free Book

If you would like to receive a FREE
copy of my psychological thriller, The Affair,
then please click the button below.

Alice Ruffalo is on the run from her violent husband. She

believes she found safety in a rundown motel in a small town.

The handsome motel clerk helps take her mind off her fears, until she starts to hear weird sounds outside her motel room and sees shadowy figures near her door.

Alice finds out the hard way that she shouldn't have stopped in this small town. Her husband knows exactly where she is.

☆☆☆☆☆ *"This is such a thrilling read." Goodreads reviewer*

☆☆☆☆☆ "A brilliant read. " Goodreads reviewer

Please email me at jamescaineauthor@gmail.com if you would like the link to my free story.

THE IN-LAWS

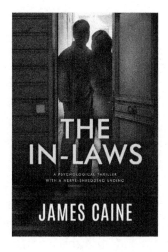

She visited them for the weekend. Now they won't let her leave.

Chelsea Jameson married the perfect husband, but he doesn't like to talk about his past.

She finds out why when his parents invite them to stay at their off-the-grid cabin in the woods.

His mother dominates his life, even though her only son is in his thirties. Her mother-in-law creates conflict and tries to manipulate her husband against Chelsea.

When Chelsea discovers more about her husband's parents, dark family secrets are unearthed, revealing the truth. This is not a regular visit to the in-laws.

Isolated and in the middle of nowhere, Chelsea needs to play their game if she wants to survive her visit.

The In-Laws is a page-turning psychological thriller that will have you guessing till the very end.

Please enjoy this sneak preview of The In-Laws:

❋ ❋ ❋

Chapter One

Martha Jameson looked one last time in Henry's room, satisfied that everything was perfect for her *son* to return to. He was finally coming home after such a long time. Everything had to be perfect when he visited.

Martha smiled. She missed him. He barely came to visit now that he was older. He has visited even less since *she* came into the picture.

Beside the bed on the nightstand was a picture of her. Chelsea. His *wife*. She had long blond hair, and large blue eyes. The picture was of her in a long-sleeved white shirt. She's only twenty-one and beaming with beauty. She's gorgeous and from what Henry says her soul is even more beautiful. This only angered Martha more. She turned the frame face down.

Martha looked across the room at a different picture frame on the dresser. She picked it up and stared at it. Martha was in her thirties when the photo was taken, and Henry was much younger. Her hand was wrapped around his shoulder. They were both smiling.

Those were different times though. Things are *different* now.

She moved the picture frame and placed it on his nightstand, replacing his wife's photo. She picked up the other frame of Chelsea and moved it to the dresser.

"Martha!" She heard his raspy voice calling for her but did not answer. She was caught up thinking about how things *used* to be. "Martha! Where are you?"

"Henry's room!" she called out to her husband. Arthur limped into the room. He grimaced in pain when he stood beside her. "Leg hurting again?" she asked.

"It's the moisture in this old home," Arthur said, sitting on Henry's bed. He made a sound of relief when he did. "Mornings are getting harder."

Martha scoffed. "I just made his bed; get off!"

He nodded and stood up, grimacing again. Arthur coughed into his flannel sleeve. 'What time are they coming?"

"Should be around supper."

Arthur cleared his throat. "Good. I need more time to get ready."

"Finish in the garden first," Martha said sternly. When she didn't hear Arthur respond, she turned to him with a cold glare. Her husband was staring off into the room. She snapped her finger at him. "Are you going to be *ready* for Henry? For— his wife? Don't mess this up."

Arthur cleared his throat and pushed his disheveled gray hair to the side. "I won't."

"We need to keep our stories straight, right?"

"Right, Martha. Of course." He wrinkled his nose and stared off into the room again to Martha's dismay.

Martha sighed. "What's her name? Do you even remember?"

Arthur cleared his throat. "Chelsea."

Martha wasn't impressed. "You're going to mess this up for us. I know it." Before her husband could respond she barked another order. "*Go*. Finish your work in the yard. I'll clean the house some more and get a salad ready from the garden for them."

Arthur didn't react as he left the room. She watched her husband limp on his left leg as he went down the hall. Time had not been kind to him. He was only sixty-five, but his body was that of a seventy-five-year-old.

Martha went down the hallway and stared out the front window. How much longer could Arthur stay out here? She had lived off the grid forever. They had their own garden, septic system, and solar panels. There were repairs to complete, maintenance tasks to stay ahead of. Could Arthur handle this lifestyle much longer? When Henry came, she would talk to him more about it.

Martha noticed a pile of white fluff surrounded by green grass outside. It was hard for her to make the white blur out, but it appeared to be moving. She took out her glasses from her dress pocket to take a closer look.

"Damnit," she said. "Not again." She tightened her lower lip as she looked at the dying chicken on the grass. She made her way outside the cabin. The grass surrounding the bird was stained with blood and feathers. The chicken moved its wings slowly. Martha picked it up by its neck and put it out of its misery with a twist.

She followed the path towards the barn where Arthur was already shoveling topsoil into a patch of small plants.

He looked at Martha and wiped the sweat from his forehead. "Chicken tonight?" He laughed to himself.

Martha was not amused. She raised its body to his face, dangling it rigorously. "That wolf is back! Set up some traps when you're done here."

He nodded. "Sure." He dug his shovel into the wheelbarrow full of soil and sprinkled it over the small plants. "Tomatoes are going to come in nicely I think."

"That wolf is going to *ruin* everything," Martha said, ignoring his comment.

"I'm almost done here," he said. "I'll put out a few traps.

It's been weeks since we saw it. It will move on again."

Martha looked down at the tomato plants. They were sprouting nicely as he said. Then she noticed a dirty finger sticking out from the ground beside a leafy plant. She shook her head as she saw several other fingers from the hand sprouting out from the soil.

"No wonder why the wolf is back," she barked, pointing at the fingers. She looked closely at one finger. An emerald ring was clearly visible on one of the blue-hued digits. Martha bent over and wrestled it off. She rubbed dirt off the band with her fingers, and spit. "You need to do a better job, Arthur," she said sternly. "Henry is coming with his wife. It needs to be perfect."

Arthur nodded, stuck his shovel in the wheelbarrow, and covered the hand with dirt until it was fully hidden.

Martha smiled thinly. If things are perfect Henry will never want to leave again.

Chapter Two

Chelsea looked out the passenger side window, taking in the woods and mountains surrounding them as Henry drove off the highway into a gas station.

"You still have half a tank," Chelsea said to her husband with a smile. "Aren't we getting close to your parents by now?" It had already been over a two-hour drive from their apartment in Calgary.

Henry smirked. "First rule: when you live out in the middle of nowhere, always gas up when you can because you may not be able to until it's too late. Learned that lesson the hard way a few times when I was younger."

Henry parked his pickup truck in front of the gasoline pump. He turned off the ignition and smirked at Chelsea again. "How about I pump, and you go inside and get a few snacks for the rest of our road trip. Grab a few of those junkie gas station brownies too, I love those. Maybe a few for my parents."

"I thought your parents lived off the land. What do they need gas bar junk brownies for?"

"They taste delicious, that's all that matters. Pretty please, sweetheart." He opened the driver side door and got out, grabbing the gas pump.

Chelsea got out of his truck and stretched her legs. She looked around at the lonely gas station on the empty road. They truly were in the middle of nowhere.

"How much longer until we get to your parents?" she asked.

Henry opened the gasket but sighed to himself as he put the pump back on the hook. "I'm getting used to the city now. They don't have pay at the pump options out here. When you go inside, can you ask them for $30 on the pump as well?"

"Sure," she said.

"And: about another hour and a half or two," he answered her with a grin.

Chelsea turned to walk towards the gas bar, but Henry whistled at her. She turned and he raised his wallet. "You may need this," he said. Chelsea put out her hand, but he waved for her to get closer, smiling.

"Stop playing games with me, Henry," she said with a laugh. "My back hurts and I want junkie gas station gummy bears as much as you want brownies." He didn't answer but kept waving her over to him.

When she was close enough, he grabbed her and pushed her against the side of the truck. He kissed her softly and leaned against her body. She could feel how *excited* he was already.

"There's something about being in the middle of nowhere with you that makes me want to tear your clothes off." he said, biting his lip.

"Stop," Chelsea said shyly. "Let's gas up, *first*." She kissed him.

He stepped back and raised her left hand, kissing her wedding band. "As you wish. Don't make me wait too long. I'm hungry... for *brownies*."

Chelsea shoved him. "You're trouble." She leaned in and kissed him again. Butterflies fluttered in her stomach every time she kissed her handsome husband.

The *honeymoon stage*, some call it. They had only been married for a few months and could barely keep their hands off each other. Even though Henry was thirty-four, he took good care of his body, and was successful, charming and funny. Sometimes Chelsea didn't understand what he saw in her. She was almost the complete opposite.

"Need gas?" an older, stockier man called out to them from the gas bar entrance. He stared at them awkwardly. "You have to pay inside."

"Sorry!" Chelsea yelled back. "Be right there."

"Why are you apologizing?" Henry whispered, raising his wallet higher.

"Stop it," Chelsea said back. "Give me the wallet." She looked back and the man was still staring at them. "He's watching."

"So what?" Henry said with a laugh.

"*Please...* give me the wallet?"

Henry lowered his hand. "Fine, I'm done playing around."

Chelsea snatched it from his hand, and when she turned to walk to the store, Henry smacked her butt. Chelsea looked back at him with an irritated face. She hated public affection like that. It was what others thought about it that bothered her most. As soon as she saw Henry's face, though, she felt nothing but his love.

"For that," she said, "I'm buying some potato chips too!" She walked towards the store and the old man went back inside the gas bar behind the counter.

She was amazed at how rustic everything was at the station. She spotted a phone booth beside the building and chuckled to herself. She couldn't remember the last time she saw a functional phone booth. She thought about going inside the booth and calling Henry from it to mess with him but decided the old man at the gas station had been waiting long enough for his only customers of the day.

When she went inside, she greeted the man behind the till, but he didn't respond. She went into the chip aisle and grabbed a few bags. She took her time going through the rest of the junk food aisle and spotted some gummy bears. Above them were the infamous brownies Henry had been craving. She grabbed a few bags and brought everything to the counter.

"Can I have thirty worth of gas, please, as well?" she asked.

The old man punched keys on his register and looked at her. "Forty-five," he said with a nasty tone. It was if her shopping in his store, with no other customers, was bothersome to him.

His curtness bothered her more. How many customers had he had today, being in the middle of nowhere? He can't smile or greet his customers? Thank them for saving his business? Instead of that happening, she paid the bill and thanked *him*.

She thought about what Henry said about the trip being another two hours potentially. She glanced around the small gas bar, looking for a washroom.

"Anything else?" the man asked.

"Is there a washroom here?"

Instead of answering he pointed at a sign. "The Outhouse is for paying customers only." Below the sign was a hook with a key on it.

"When you're done using it, lock the door," he said.

"Never mind," Chelsea said with a smile. "Thanks." She turned to leave and saw a billboard beside the exit door. Although the board was small it was stacked with missing persons posters. Some were piled on top of each other.

Chelsea glanced at a few posters. It amazed her to think all the pictures of the people on this board were missing. Someone out there was looking for them and they couldn't be found. How many of them were alive? How many were only runaways, who wanted to stay missing for their own reasons? She hoped for most of these people it was the latter.

She noticed a weathered poster tacked underneath two others. Caroline Sanders. She had been missing for over two years. Last seen hiking the Grassi Lakes Trail in Kananaskis Country. At the bottom of the page was a case number and phone number to call with any information.

Chelsea took her time looking at the rest of the board at all the missing faces staring back at her. Most of them were older men and women, with a few exceptions.

"Do you want to buy some lottery tickets?" the old man asked.

"What?" Chelsea said.

The old man nodded at the lottery station below the missing persons board. "Just fill out your lucky numbers and maybe you could be the next one who wins. You saw that winning ticket on the board?"

Chelsea looked up at the board again. Below the posters of a few women was a picture of a lottery ticket. Handwritten, with poor lettering, were the words "$25,000 Winner."

"That could be you," the old man said with an ugly leer.

Chelsea was annoyed. The board of these missing people was desecrated with this man's greed. No wonder the missing stay vanished.

"I'm not that lucky," Chelsea said. She left the store without saying goodbye to the cashier. To her that was the worst thing she could do to someone, leave without acknowledging them. To the old man, he could care less if he ever saw her again – or if her face was on the bulletin board some day.

"Excuse me, miss." Chelsea turned to see a young boy with pudgy cheeks on a red bicycle. Chelsea assumed he was around ten years old. His face was flushed red. Another boy who looked younger was sitting on a blue bike nearby.

"Yes?" Chelsea said with a smile.

"Well, I think we are a little lost," he said, lowering his head. "My mom told me not to go too far, but we didn't listen. Do you have a phone? Could I call her to come by and pick us up?"

"Of course." She took out her cell from her jean pocket and looked at the screen, noticing a new text from her friend Neil. She quickly read it.

"In-laws making you go crazy yet?" it read. Chelsea rolled her eyes.

She gave the phone to the boy on the bicycle. "Here you go."

The boy looked up at her. "The screen's locked though."

Chelsea waved her hand at him. "There isn't a password. Just swipe to open it. Do you want me to show you how to call someone?"

The boy put the phone in his pocket. He turned his bike toward the road and jumped on the pedals. His friend on the blue bike was already starting to head off fast.

"Hey!" Chelsea yelled at the boy. "Stop!"

The boy on the red bicycle was laughing as he pedaled until Henry ran in front of him and knocked him off his bike. Henry quickly grabbed the boy and picked him up from the ground gently, but forcefully. Henry wiped dirt off the boy's clothes from the fall. He reached into the kid's pocket, grabbed the cell phone, and let go of the boy.

"Scram, kid," he said with a stern look. He watched as the boy picked up his bike and slowly started pedaling towards his friend on the road.

"Mike!" the boy yelled. "Wait for me!"

Henry looked back at Chelsea and slowly walked up to her; his hand stretched out with her phone. "I believe this is yours."

"I can't believe that happened," she said with a look of concern. "Those were, well, *bad boys*. Who does that?" She took her phone from his hand and opened it to make sure it wasn't broken. She was relieved when she saw it was fine.

Henry smiled. "When you move to Toronto, you better not be this gullible. That city will break you."

"Maybe we should call the cops?" Chelsea said, ignoring his comment.

"No, I lived in small towns my whole life. These boys are just *bored*. Thought you were an easy target."

"I'm not gullible!" she said. "The boy said he was lost. He needed my phone. I didn't want him to end up... on a missing persons poster."

Henry smirked. "*Gullible*," he repeated. He looked down at the junk food on the ground. He bent over and picked up a smooshed brownie. "Now, this is a *tragedy*."

Chelsea waved her head. "I'm not going back inside that gas station to get another one! That old man inside is the worst, and so are those kids."

Henry grabbed her hand and kissed her wedding band. "Gullible and too sweet for your own good. If that old man was mean to you, you should tell him."

"He wasn't mean. He just... wasn't nice. I'm not that kind of girl to tell people what I think, you know that," Chelsea said, shoving him playfully. "That's why I married you."

Chapter Three

Chelsea finished the last of her snacks as Henry pulled onto a dirt road off the highway.

"About another twenty minutes," he said, taking a sip of his warm cola. He turned his head to look at Chelsea and with one hand sternly on the wheel, he brushed his hand against the side of her face.

Chelsea welcomed his touch, even though she hated the gritty feel of his sandpaper fingers. For someone who was very successful, he had the hands of a man who worked physical labor every day of his life.

Before being a successful business owner, Henry did have a hard life. From what he was willing to tell her about him growing up, she knew it was difficult. His father built the cabin in Kananaskis Country, int the middle of nowhere, moving his whole life into the woods, dragging Henry with him. Henry was forced to drop out of high school and was taught at home by his mother. He had no prom, no best friends, only his parents.

It wasn't until he was old enough to demand more from his life that his parents let him leave. Henry said when he was seventeen and set out to live his own life, it was almost as if he went into a different world when he left the woods.

It was also difficult to find work without your high school diploma. He found stable work as a security guard and worked his way up to manager of the company within five years. Soon, an opportunity came to buy the company itself, and he took it. Now he owned and operated Secure Surveillance, one of the largest local security companies in the province.

Chelsea always admired that about him, his *drive*. He'd gone from being a jungle boy out in the woods to being head of the company and business owner, of it all within a handful of years.

Chelsea was twenty-one, and still figuring out life. She was a struggling painter, trying to have her paintbrush make

THE PATIENT'S LIST: A GRIPPING PSYCHOLOGICAL THRILLER WITH A KILL...

a mark. When her friend Neil said he was going to go to a prestigious arts program at the University of Toronto, and asked her to join, she knew this was her opportunity, and like Henry she planned on taking it.

Henry didn't like it though.

The car started to slow as Henry rolled past a chain link fence. A large wood pole was cut in half, the other part face down in the grass below it. Soon they entered a wide, empty dirt parking lot.

Henry parked his truck. "We're here."

Chelsea smirked, waiting for him to say something that made sense. Instead, he turned off the ignition, and stepped out of the driver's seat. He stretched out his arms and moaned.

"What are you talking about Henry?" Chelsea shouted. "We're in the middle of nowhere."

Henry walked to the back of the truck, lowering the bed and taking out Chelsea's backpack. "I told you, that's where they live, in the middle of nowhere." He pointed towards a grouping of trees. "We have to go about four hours that way." He looked back at Chelsea with a smile, but she didn't return it. "What?" he said. "I'm not messing with you, it is!"

Chelsea sighed. "What did I sign up for?"

"A whole weekend of *fun!*" Henry answered with enthusiasm.

"It feels like it took a whole weekend to get here."

"And just four more hours to go." Henry handed her her backpack and Chelsea wrapped it around her shoulders. Henry put his on, and shut his truck bed, locking his vehicle with his fob key.

They walked for an hour into the woods. Chelsea tried to keep things lighthearted, but she was annoyed at Henry. Usually, when frustrated with someone, that person would never know that Chelsea felt hurt, but Henry was the only person to whom she was ever able to say what was on her mind. It was the reason she fell for him quickly. She felt safe with him. She could open up to him, about her life, everything she had gone through.

She lost her mother at a young age, and during the past year, her father as well from a heart attack. Henry was with her the whole time. He saw and understood her emotions, sometimes better than she did.

"Are you going to tell me?" he asked. Henry ducked under a low-lying tree branch and looked back at her. As Chelsea reached the branch, he lifted it for her until she was through. "You're upset? Is it because I dragged you out in the middle of nowhere to meet my parents?"

"No," Chelsea said, lowering her head. "You don't really think *poorly* of me, do you?"

"What do you mean?"

"*Gullible*? I mean, you don't think I'm *stupid*, right?"

Henry stopped walking and grabbed her hand softly. "No, I don't. I think the world of you. Gullible was… the wrong word to use. You're… just a good person. Some people try to take advantage of that."

Chelsea nodded. "Those boys could have needed help."

"I take it when you left the store, you didn't see the one on the red bicycle slip his cell phone in his other pocket?"

Chelsea furrowed her eyebrows. She didn't. How many people have those boys tricked? she thought to herself. She remembered the missing people on the board in the gas bar. "Well, that doesn't matter," she said. "Maybe their cell died, and they needed help. Sometimes people need help, and need good people, like me."

"You're right. Maybe I think too negatively of people. I'm… sorry, okay?" He wrapped his hand around her waist and pulled Chelsea towards him, kissing her gently. "I mean it."

Chelsea smiled. "That's why I love you, Henry. You can admit to things. Please, don't ever change."

Chelsea held his hand tight. She remembered something her father told her, in his last few months while in the hospital recovering from another heart attack. "That man is special, Sea," he told her. Sea was a nickname he'd had for her for as long as she could remember. Her father had told Chelsea that her eyes were like her mother's and were as blue as the Atlantic. Her father didn't say it, but she knew he wanted to see her get married. She was his only child. She had dreamed of him walking her down the aisle, but with his deteriorating health, knew it wouldn't happen.

One night on a random date, Henry surprised her with a party at her favourite restaurant with friends and her father waiting. That night he proposed.

She covered her mouth in shock when Henry got down on one knee. Although they had only been together for six months, she was already head over heels for him. After he asked for her hand in marriage, Chelsea quickly looked at her father, who nodded in agreement. Soon after, her father's health began deteriorating further. Chelsea and Henry initially planned to have their wedding at a church with a large party after, but none of that mattered to her anymore. Like every girl, Chelsea had dreamed about what her wedding day would be like, and she had big plans for it, but if her father wasn't there, it wouldn't have mattered.

Henry agreed to have the wedding within two months, and they were able to quickly get everything in order. Chelsea's father did walk her down the aisle. In the end she did have the wedding she wanted because the people she cared about most were with her.

Unfortunately, Henry's parents weren't able to attend. Chelsea hadn't even met her in-laws until this weekend. When Chelsea asked why they couldn't come, Henry rolled his eyes, telling her how particular they were. They hadn't left their cabin in the woods in years. Henry would bring anything they requested to them, if they needed anything, which was rare.

A month after the wedding, Chelsea's father passed.

Now it had been almost four months since he died. She grieved for her father but was starting to see the other side of her heartbreak.

Henry was with her the whole time, and she loved him even more for it. She felt bad for not being the newlywed wife he had dreamed of. Instead, she was a tearful mess. Now she was getting her life back on track, though. Now she wanted to go to art school in Toronto, and after, focus on her life with her husband, and maybe even a few kids along the way.

Chelsea got her foot stuck in some mud for a moment and twisted it out. She looked around at the dense woods surrounding them. How did Henry even know where to go? There was no discernable path. When she asked him, he said he knew these woods like the back of his hand. All she saw were trees and bushes, but they were like road signs to Henry.

"I thought you were used to camping as a kid?" he said.

"My father always took me," she said, "but nothing like this. We went to popular camps, and when he was older, we would rent RVs. Nothing off the grid, like you or your parents."

"Make sure to tell my parents that," he said. "The last girl I brought to them didn't know a lick about being out in the woods."

Chelsea laughed. "Here I was thinking I was the only girl you brought out in the middle of nowhere."

"Only a few I brought home to the parents," Henry said. He looked back at Chelsea and smiled. "They are going to love you."

Henry had said that a few times already on their trip. The more he said it, the more pressure she felt. What if they *hated* her?

She had assumed his parents were the type to not want to be around people, given their chosen lifestyle. She had asked to meet them several times, but only now was Henry able to make it happen.

"I'm happy I finally get to meet them," she answered.

"It's the perfect weekend for it, too," Henry said. "I've got a huge project starting soon. It's going to be super busy. You have art school potentially starting in a week. Before all these hectic things happen, we get to spend some quality time with my folks."

Chelsea felt bitter when he said "*potentially*" going to art

THE PATIENT'S LIST: A GRIPPING PSYCHOLOGICAL THRILLER WITH A KILL...

school. She wasn't sure what he hated more, the idea of her leaving the province or her going to school with Neil. They had talked/argued about it many times over the past month. Henry felt she was rushing into something, but Chelsea knew she was ready to start her life again. Neil wasn't a sexual threat to Henry. Since the first time they kissed, Chelsea only had eyes for her husband. With his looks and charm, it wasn't too hard to maintain. Neil, on the other hand, was just *Neil.* nothing more than a good friend.

Chelsea thought about saying something but didn't want to argue about it.

"Are we almost there?" she asked.

Henry nodded. "About an hour or so left."

"Ugh. I have to pee!"

Henry looked around the woods. "Pick your potty."

"An hour?" she repeated. "Fine!"

"What?" Henry laughed. "When you were in the Beavers when you were younger, you didn't go pee outside?"

"Beavers was for little boys. *Girl Guides* were for girls," she corrected.

Chelsea found a large tree and went out of sight from Henry. She pulled down her jeans and panties, and cautiously looked around before releasing. She hovered over a pile of leaves and felt a flick of urine on the side of her legs, making her wince. A sound of crunching leaves getting closer made her almost jump.

"Henry!" she yelled. "Can a girl get some privacy around here?"

The crunching sound stopped.

From a distance, Henry began shouting, "Eh Bear! Go Bear! Go!"

Chelsea froze. She heard movement from a bush near her, and the sound of something whizzing off into the woods.

Henry ran up to her. "Are you okay?"

"Was that a bear?" Chelsea managed to say between deep breaths.

"I'm not sure," Henry said. "It was something *big*. It's gone now."

"Oh boy!" Chelsea said, taking a deep breath.

"Didn't they teach you in Girl Guides that most of the animals out in the woods are more scared of you then you are of them?" He reached out his hand and Chelsea grabbed it. "Let's hurry up. We can get there soon."

It took Chelsea some time to shrug off what happened, but when she found her pace again, they got to their destination. They soon made it to an area free of bushes and trees. She spotted the roof of a wood barn.

"Oh, thank god," Chelsea exclaimed. Henry laughed.

A fence made with wood and nails surrounded a large clearing. They followed a dirt path that went to the gate. Henry lifted the latch to open it, and Chelsea noticed a large sign tacked to the fence that read "Do Not Trespass" and another below it that read "Property Under Video Surveillance."

They walked down the path that led to a large one-storey cabin. Chelsea's father would have loved a place like this. He would have enjoyed booking a vacation at a cabin in the woods. She couldn't imagine living here year-round, though.

"You should see the large garden in the back," Henry said. 'I'm sure my parents will show you. They're so proud of it."

Chelsea did enjoy gardening. She'd had a small tomato plant at their apartment in Calgary but somehow killed it within a few days.

Henry walked up the wood stairs to the front door, with Chelsea taking her time behind him. He knocked and waited.

Chelsea noticed a camera on the porch facing them. Henry answered her before she could ask.

"Runs on a generator," he said. "I installed their whole system. It's amazing what you can do now."

Chelsea nodded and waited anxiously for the door to open. She heard no movement from inside the home. She peeked inside a window and saw three fabric chairs sitting beside a metal fireplace. There were no lights on inside, or movement.

Henry knocked on the door again, harder. "Mom! Dad!" he yelled. After another minute of waiting, he looked at Chelsea. "I guess they're not home. Maybe we should go back to the truck and come back a different time?" When Chelsea didn't react to his joke, he laughed to himself. "They could be in the garden." Henry waved at Chelsea to follow him down the porch steps, but then she heard a creak at the front door.

It slowly opened, and a woman dressed in a black dress to her knees stepped out. Henry has told her she was in her early fifties but could easily have passed for a woman in her forties. Her thick, dark eyebrows raised when she saw Henry.

"Henry!" She wrapped her arms around him tight. "Please, come inside. Your father and I have been waiting all day!" She forcefully grabbed him and guided him inside.

Henry shouted, "Dad!"

Chelsea smiled to herself, taking in the moment of seeing Henry reunite with his family.

His mother noticed her. Immediately her face, once bright with happiness, slumped to a more neutral demeanour.

"You must be Chelsea," she said to her daughter-in-law. Before Chelsea could answer, Henry's mother turned from her and gestured for her to follow. "Come inside!" she yelled to Chelsea.

* * *

Ladybird, ladybird fly away home,

Your house is on fire and your children are gone,

All except one, and her name is Amy,

And she hid under the baking pan.

Printed in Great Britain
by Amazon

16239250R00129